First Published Worldwide 2016

Copyright © Luke Smitherd 2001

Cover artwork by Luke Smitherd

ISBN 9781519045515

Books By Luke Smitherd:

<u>Full-Length Novels:</u>

The Physics Of The Dead

The Stone Man

A Head Full Of Knives

Weird. Dark.

How To Be A Vigilante: A Diary

Kill Someone

<u>Novellas</u>

The Man On Table Ten

Hold On Until Your Fingers Break

My Name Is Mister Grief

He Waits

Do Anything

For an up-to-date list of Luke Smitherd's other books, his blog, YouTube clips and more, visit www.lukesmitherd.com

Acknowledgements

At the time of writing, the following people wrote a nice Amazon or Audible (.com or co.uk) review of *How To Be A Vigilante: A Diary*. Thank you so, so much. As someone still fairly unknown in the book writing game, those reviews mean everything. I'm only using the names you put on your reviews, as these will be ones you're happy to have associated with my work... I hope:

451, A. D. Hall, Abigailspider, Adams family, AgirlWaiting, airhugs, Alexandra, Amazon Customer, Angel Colin, Angela Wallis, Anne, AudiobookFan, Bakerstreet, Barbra, Beet Nixon, Big, BigDog, bladerunner, Blanchepadgett, Bodornic, BoneyD, Book Thief, booknerdsbraindump, Booky Lorra, BSM, CaryLory, cat payton, Cherrie Hacney, cheryl, chrisbobs, CJ, Claireyclaireyclaire, Cliffnook2000, ConMar62, Crippsy, Damo, DaveC, David Plank, DavidAllan, Dc Fitzgerald, Don, Drew, Drucilla(Drac)Buckley, Elliot Brown, Emil Despodov, Emma Shawcross, G. Parlee, Garry M, Ged Byrne, Gex, Gilaine, Glen Gilchrist, Gotan the reader, H. J. Battle, Heidi, helen, Henry, I. Burke, J M Dho, Jacque Ledoux, James Liston, Jamie Greenwood, Jan Fisher Sylvester, Janice Clark, Jason goldsmid, Jason Jones, Jayg324, jek, Jeremy A. Smith, Jinny, JoanneG, John Mitchell, Jon Perry, Jonny Barr, Julian Bosley, Julie Blaskie, Julja, K. Edwin Fritz, author, katrina, Kelly G, Kelly Howard, Kelly Jobes, Kelly Rickard, Kelly Woodward, L. Durden, Lauren, Lorna, Louise Smith, LouiseTheFox, M. Iddon, M. King, madalyn king, Mark Fowler, Mark Ledsom, Mark Say, Megan Hodgkins, melissamcke, MetalHead, Michael Bigwood, Michelle Kennedy, Mike Nolan, Milking Badger, Miss S. A. Munn, Mr, Mr J Whiterod, Mr. Anthony Grayson, Mr. Damian M. Sears, Mr Lee Hopkins, Mr Matt Norgrove, Mr C., Mr. C. F. Gilbert, Mrs Hill, Mrs Kindle, Neil, Nita V. Jester-Frantz, P W R Wilcox, P. Conde, P.S. Stephenson, Pamela Goodlad, Pammarshall04, paul, PAUL DENNIS, Paul Hopkinson, Paul Korhonen, Pixel, prettyace, R. GILL, Rachel Jane, Rebekah Jones, Robert, Robert S Kaplan, Roger G, Rosalie Jenifer James, Russ, Ryuto, Sarah H, SciFiFan, Seamus Bopster, Silversmith, Simon, simon211175, Sir Lister, Steph in Nottingham, Stephen, Steve Blencowe, Steven, stu_999, Sue Phillips, swebby, Tamsin White, tejadab, TerryF, The Dogs Mum, The Fro, Tino1440, TonyM, trev, Troy Linehan, Uncle Lou, UnionJack, valkyrie, Weez, wrayfish, Yetiish

Patreon Posse:
Michelle McDonald, Mike Hands, Patricia Mussone, Frank Larocca, Sherry Diehr, Dean Bones, Michelle Kennedy, Rob Dennis, Marty Brastow, Steve Blencowe, Becky Brock, Glenn Curtis, Pete Hughes, K. Edwin Fritz, Kathy Logan, James Phoenix, Barbra Smerz, Richard Carnes, Jeremy Smith, Jayme Erickson, and Barbara Haynes.

Sincere thanks to Sophie, Henna, and Laurence at Audible for giving me my first big break. It won't ever be forgotten.

Current list of Smithereens with Titles (see afterword on how to get yours):

Emil: King of the Macedonian Smithereens; Neil Novita: Chief Smithereen of Brooklyn; Jay McTyier: Derby City Smithereen; Ashfaq Jilani: Nawab of the South East London Smithereens; Jason Jones: Archduke of lower Alabama; Betty Morgan: President of Massachusetts Smithereens; Malinda Quartel Qoupe: Queen of the Sandbox (Saudi Arabia); Marty Brastow: Grand Poobah of the LA Smithereens; John Osmond: Captain Toronto; Nita Jester Franz: Goddess of the Olympian Smithereens; Angie Hackett: Keeper of Du; Colleen Cassidy: The Tax Queen Smithereen; Jo Cranford: The Cajun Queen Smithereen; Gary Johnayak: Captain of the Yellow Smithereen; Matt Bryant: the High Lord Dominator of South Southeast San Jose; Rich Gill: Chief Executive Smithereen - Plymouth Branch; Sheryl: Shish the Completely Sane Cat Lady of Silver Lake; Charlie Gold: Smithereen In Chief Of Barnet; Gord Parlee: Prime Transcendent Smithereen, Vancouver Island Division; Erik Hundstad: King Smithereen of Norway(a greedy title but I've allowed it this once); Sarah Hirst: Official Smithereen Knitter of Nottingham; Christine Jones: Molehunter Smithereen Extraordinaire, Marcie Carole Spencer: Princess Smithereen of Elmet, and Angela Wallis: Chief Smithereen of Strathblanefield.

Kill Someone

By

Luke Smitherd

For Oxley

Part One: The Pitch

"To have dominion you must have a genius for organising." - John Henry Newman

Chapter One: The Man in White, The Dangers Of Video Conferencing, and Some Very Important Rules and Regulations

***

When I was still truly young, The Man in White came to my family's house on a cold Saturday morning in November. Klaus – although his name was not yet Klaus – was, of course, with him.

At twenty-one years old, I really *was* a young man, and I don't mean in terms of age. I mean my *attitude*, compared to those around me who'd been in my year at school. Although I wouldn't admit it at the time, I knew it deep down. It was probably why I was still working in a shit job three years after graduating and not attending university. I knew I would have crashed out halfway through the first year. In many ways, I think taking that shitty agency job was my first honest-to-god attempt at being an adult, but I could have worked there for twenty years and I don't think I'd have handled things any better. I try to think of any *adults* I've known that would have been able to handle what that man had to tell me, and I can't. I reckon they would have to have been psychopaths to do so, and as far as I'm aware, I didn't know any.

Of course, I often think about what happened – every day, as you'd expect, but I mean I ask myself, specifically, if I have any regrets. That's a difficult question to answer because there's regret and then there's *culpable* regret, you see. Active regret, to me, means things that I felt I handled badly, or wrong choices I made *for the wrong reasons,* you know? Like sleeping in an hour longer when you know you shouldn't, or eating that extra dessert when you know you want to lose weight. Those are *culpable* regrets.

For the most part, I know I at least made choices I *thought* were right; what I thought were the best possible choices at the time. But was I truly culpable? Can I be culpable when faced with an *impossible* choice? I've never truly known. Not even once in the many, many long nights that have followed.

The very last choice, of course. The one that will never, ever leave me, no matter how much I try to make up for it. That's why I'm writing this journal; to at least purge *some* of the crap inside me. To fill the Microsoft Word equivalent of paper on a cheap-ass laptop - bought solely for this purpose - that will never, *ever*, be connected to the internet. Can't have any hack-happy assholes finding out about this.

That son of a bitch. That son of a bitch and his grinning face.

That morning – following the last day of my life that was still fully my own - the crappy old doorbell at my parents' house woke me from a deep sleep. It took me a minute or two to figure out what was going on. What was the strange drilling sound? Then my cognitive process caught up with reality, the *brrrrrrrrrrrr* of the doorbell demanding an answer.

Someone has a problem. Maybe I've done something wrong. No, someone's broken down out here, that's it. The only reason someone's calling this *early is because we're the only house around here.*

The last part was true, at least. As I dragged my bleary-eyed carcass out of bed, the startling and surprising whiteness from the fields outside hurt my eyes as it penetrated the thin bedroom curtains. It had snowed during the night, apparently. The rolling countryside around my parents' farm (inactive) turned into a dazzlingly harsh whiteness that would be a wonderland to some and an eye-stinging nightmare to first-thing-in-the-morning Chris Summer.

"Hang on..." I called, grabbing my moth-eaten robe from the hook on the bedroom door and angrily thrusting my arms into it. I had a right to be angry, didn't I? That was a rough time for me. I spent endless days at the call centre and spent the rest of the time being constantly *knackered.* It was frankly a miracle that I never got fired, such a zombie was I on a daily basis. I was rarely asleep before 2 am, despite my best efforts, and the weekends were my only chance to catch up. On that particular morning, I knew I'd never get back to sleep again, and—

Brrrrrrrrrrrrrrrrrrrrrrrrrrrrrrrrrrrrrrrrrrrrrrrrrrrrrrrrrrrrrrrrrrr.

Now *that* pissed me off. I froze. What the fuck? Someone leaning on the doorbell like that? Who the hell did they think they were? I was suddenly torn between going back to bed just to ignore such rudeness, and a desire to go downstairs and give the business to whoever was treating my doorbell like some sort of servant-summoning device. In my angry, sleep-frustrated state, I chose the latter. I flung the bedroom door open and pounded my way down the narrow wooden staircase, reached the front door, and gave *that* door the flinging treatment, too. The brisk late autumn air hit me as a very terse and above-normal-volume *yes?* was in the process of passing my lips... but one that petered out when I saw the strange sight in front of me. The *yes?* ended up as simply,

"Yfff ..."

In hindsight, when I think about what I was going to say—that I was going to give *those* guys the roasting and have them scared of *me*—I almost laugh at the ridiculousness of it.

A smiling man was standing in front of my parents' doorstep, with a very large and *un*smiling man standing immediately behind him. The gravel yard outside, with the chickens milling about (the only animals on the entire property, other than the cat, due to my parents' fondness for fresh eggs) and the thin layer of snow made the image of the two men before me seem even more surreal. This was because the large man in his black suit and shades stood out in such contrast to the whiteness, and because the smaller man almost blended into it with his white suit, shirt, tie, and grey hair. Both of them wore leather gloves and sunglasses.

The white-suited man's smile was so wide as to be almost unsettling, and the crisp neatness of the suit surrounded by the farm setting was just... *weird*. He was about my height of 5'9", but a good deal older, perhaps in his early fifties. His skin was pale, but he still looked healthy and robust. His smile certainly was. The large man behind him was slowly scanning the exterior of the house, the courtyard, and the distance off to the left. Everything about him—his close-cropped blond hair, black sunglasses, his bulk, his chiseled face, the way he was dressed—said *Spook.*

What... the hell...?

"Chris Summer?" the man in the white suit asked me, extending a hand. I shook it, feeling the leather in mine, any thoughts of outrage already blasted away. I was immediately *very* nervous. Who could blame me? I mean, who has people like this turn up on their doorstep this early on a Saturday morning? This was already *extremely* fucking weird. All of it: they knew my name; the sheer size and formal dress of the large man; this guy's white suit... Were they drug guys? Had somebody said something to someone? I would occasionally smoke the odd joint, but I never ran with anybody that was really into that kind of thing. My heart rate was already up and my scalp felt loose.

"Yes..." I said, suddenly feeling very vulnerable and foolish in my scabby old robe. Also, cold. The crisp, chill air was moving around my bare ankles and bony toes. "Uh... I don't think I..." The Man in White held up a hand, smiling, and cocked his head away slightly. *No need,* the gesture said. *I know this is a surprise.*

"I understand, Mr. Summer," he said. "This is out of the blue, I know. I also know this is very early for a house call, but I wanted to make sure you were in. We woke you up by the looks of it. Sorry about that."

"That's... fine."

"May I call you Chris?"

Who the fuck is this guy?

Thoughts of slamming the door and calling the police were clamouring inside my head. You'd be thinking the same thing, right? Was this a dream? I didn't want to get into a discussion and thought it a very bad idea to get drawn into one, but just as I was about to close the door, I had a vision of the Mr. Black Ops out there busting through it.

Would he do that?

They clearly came here at 7 am to talk to you. Did you really think they're just going to leave?

What the hell is going on?

I tried to summon up some internal solidity. I've never been a tough guy, and I knew that the big unit would easily eat me for breakfast, but my father had always told me never to show weakness in a potentially dangerous situation. *If you do, Chris, you're already screwed.* I had to stand up a little bit, if only until I could get my head around the situation.

"Well... I mean... that depends on what this is about," I said, shifting on my feet, partially due to nerves and partially from the cold.

"Well, I'm not going to lie to you, Chris," the Man in White said, "what I have to tell you is highly unusual. Pretty weird, certainly. Very weird. And look, I'll be honest, you're probably not going to like it. But the *good* news is that we will leave you alone the second you say so, but I would really recommend - for your own peace of mind - at least hearing what I have to say."

I felt my blood run that much colder. Not just because of the terrifying phrase *you're probably not going to like it,* but because of something even more simple. It was far more subtle, yet hit me the hardest: he was using my first name. He'd asked if he could, I hadn't given my permission, but he hadn't waited for an answer. It didn't matter to him. I wanted to say just that, *I didn't give you my permission,* but it just felt like a strange thing to say - impolite.

That's bullshit. If I can't be honest now, what's the point in even thinking about this?

I didn't say anything because, at that moment, I was scared shitless.

"Why won't I like it? Who are you?" I asked. *Who are you* sounds like quite a confrontational and perhaps brave thing to say, but believe me, it wasn't delivered in that manner. I stammered as I said it.

"May we come in and tell you?" the Man in White asked, with a theatrical, hey-here's-a-crazy-idea shrug, the world's least convincing used car salesman. "Again, we'll leave as soon as you say, but you will want to hear this." His voice was so ordinary, so-straight-out-of-a-dentist's-office, that it was almost disarming.

I looked at the hulk behind him, looked at the Man in White's permagrin, and heard the words leave my mouth on autopilot. Fear response.

"No," I said. "No... I don't know who you are." I felt my legs start to tremble as I said it, scarcely believing that I was disobeying. I'd read about that happening in books, but here it was happening to me for real. I wouldn't be able to stand if this went on much longer. I'd been asleep three minutes ago; how was it possible that I was in this situation already? "I think I want you to leave, actually. I want you to go away." I could taste copper on my breath. The Man in White's grin faltered a little, but just a little.

"Well, listen Chris, that's fine," he said, holding up his hands. "I said we'd leave if you asked us to leave, and I'm under very, very strict instructions to give you total freedom here."

Give *me total freedom?* I thought. *You don't give me total freedom! You don't give me anything! I already have total freedom and it isn't up to you!* That had really made me angry, but not angry enough to actually say it. *Under instructions? Under instructions from who?*

"But listen, I think you should at least know what's at stake," the Man in White continued, "and then you'll be better informed. I'd feel very bad indeed if you didn't know the whole score, as I'm almost certain that if you did, you wouldn't want us to leave. Not because of any problems you would experience – you will experience *no* problems from us, directly or indirectly, and neither will anyone you know, but because I'm sure you're a good person and a good person would *want* to know, or he'd want to know if, ah, he knew the situation, if that makes sense." The last part was said with a little chuckle, like a light joke given in the middle of a lecture.

"What situation?" I asked, both desperate to know and not wanting to know at all.

The Man in White's smile vanished from his face, like it was a living thing that had somehow been instantly shot dead.

"Someone is going to die if you don't talk to us, Chris. Several someones, in fact. No one you know personally, but human beings, nonetheless. My employer's associates already have them, and if you don't hear us out, they will kill them."

There was silence then, broken only by the light breeze blowing in my ears.

The Man in White's gaze bored into me, his eyes hidden behind his sunglasses.

The huge man behind him stared at me too, his scanning halted, *his* eyes hidden behind *his sun*glasses.

All I could think was:

This is a joke. Or a dream. It has *to be a dream.*

"That's all you have to do, Chris, to save these lives," the Man in White said. "Hear us out. And then if you don't want any further part of this, we'll leave. Of course, you could say you want no further part of this *right now,* but people will die."

This is bullshit. This is too crazy to be real. It doesn't matter what these guys look like. This is bullshit.

The Man in White looked over his shoulder briefly to the unit standing behind him and nodded his head towards me. I flinched, suddenly expecting an attack, but one of the large man's leather-gloved hands slowly emerged from behind his back holding an iPad. He took off one glove, revealing an enormous mitt of a hand, and pressed a thumb over the tablet's thumbprint lock. Once satisfied, his expressionless face came up as he turned the tablet outwards to face me.

On the screen was a video of five young women, on their knees, lined up in a row inside a darkened room. They were all wearing blindfolds. One of them was crying, one of them was calling to her repeating *it's ok, its ok,* while the others were just breathing, steadily. That's what I remember most clearly. The way they were visibly trying to stay calm.

I looked at the image on the tablet, looked at the blank black windows of the Man in White's sunglasses and his expressionless face, and looked back at the tablet. The big man's hand moved in front of the iPad, tapping the screen and bringing up a bunch of options. When I saw the onscreen menu appear, I realized this was some kind of video calling app, which meant that this was live.

Bullshit... bullshit... what the fuck...?

"They can't see you, don't worry," the Man in White said, as the bigger man's finger tapped the microphone symbol on the screen. "But they can hear you now."

The only sound around my parents' doorstep was that coming from the tablet. The screen, the sunglasses, back to the screen.

"Who... what are you doing?" I began, needing something, *anything*, to break that moment of sudden and horrifying inertia, to try and snap back into a reality I understood, when every single girl on that screen suddenly became alert and straightened up. I heard my own voice echo back slightly from the speakers after a half-second delay, hearing my own voice echoing off the walls of a room I had never entered. All the girls started shouting at once.

"Who's there, who's that, let us out, please, help us, help us—"

I couldn't speak. I couldn't move. I could only listen to that terrified babble, a cacophony of fear and desperation.

This was real.

The iPad screen went blank, and the sound was cut off abruptly as the large man pressed the lock button. The tablet went away, and there was silence again as I stood trembling on the doorstep, holding onto the frame for support. The Man in White stood still, his black sunglasses like the eyes of a fly, and silent, as if waiting for a response from me. After a moment or two, the smile started to creep back onto his face. It was horrible to watch, like seeing an infection work its way across someone's skin.

"These young women, to be precise," he said. "Again, no one you know, but people nonetheless. Perhaps you've heard of these five? They've been on the news quite a lot. I'd be surprised if you hadn't, really."

No way, I thought, something making sense in a moment of utter horror. *No fucking way. The MacArthur Quintuplets.* Now that they'd told me, I realized I recognized the girls even behind the blindfolds. I'd known their famous faces even before their disappearances had been all over every hysterical news outlet in the country.

Alan MacArthur was and still is a local businessman who had done very, very well for himself. A billionaire no less, taking his parents' small chain of hotels and expanding it nationally, then growing the MacArthur brand to encompass gyms and nursing homes. He was famous for being a family man, backing after school programs and, more famously, having five daughters. They weren't *actual* quintuplets. Three of them *were* triplets, and the other two had come so soon after that, whenever the papers ran a story on the family, the Q-bomb was dropped. It stuck. The youngest was now 22. The eldest three, 23.

They had a brother too, one who was a good five years older than them, but despite resurfacing when the girls had been taken—standing quietly with his parents at the press conferences and appeals to the kidnappers—he didn't normally do the whole "society scene". But the girls famously did more than that. While glamorous (the press never tired of trying to link them to various male celebrities), they were well-known philanthropists, working tirelessly for child protection and animal charities.

They'd been abducted a week ago during a fundraiser at a cricket ground. The papers had said that the kidnapping must have been particularly audacious, as the abductors would have had to take one girl, unseen, and kept coming back for the others. *Considerable resources,* a police statement had said. (I looked the police responses up later. I did a *lot* of looking things up once the whole sorry mess was said and done.) They'd managed to stay out-of-sight of the small number of CCTV cameras, particularly since most of the event was occurring on the out-of-season pitch. Nobody had seen anything. Nobody had reported anything. No one was even sure there was a problem until twenty-four hours had passed and Alan MacArthur's daughters hadn't come home. All five of their phones went straight to the answering service.

The story had, of course, gone national, with all of the usual accompanying media madness and analysis, but the girls had stayed missing, and the leads appeared to be few.

My wide, trembling eyes travelled from one set of sunglasses to another, meeting the gaze of the large man standing behind my early morning visitor. I took him in again; my initial suspicions proved quite right.

Of course there were no leads. Men like him don't leave trails.

I felt my legs completely go, suddenly and without warning, but caught the doorframe again, white-knuckled this time. The Man in White actually darted forward for a moment to catch me but pulled up short when he realized I wouldn't fall.

You are now a part of this, I thought to myself. *The girls. The news. Now you know who has them. They're right here; they're showing you. What the fuck is this? What are they going to do to you—*

"Chris, listen to me," the Man in White was saying, holding up both hands as if to say *whatever you're worrying about, it's ok.* "We mean it. Even though you've seen us, trust me, you could tell the cops *everything.* They'd never find us. Our employer can fix anything even if they did. He's connected. So you. Are. Safe. Ok?"

"Did you... did you..." I stammered, feeling as if I couldn't take in any air.

"Not me personally, I'll be honest," the Man in White said, sounding impatient. "Our associates did. Look, it's really cold out here, and I've promised you all I can promise. All you have to do is hear us out and then we'll go. If you don't, one of those five girls dies immediately. They're nobody to you. I understand that, but even so, a life is a life. Is not listening to me talk for a few minutes worth somebody's life? And look."

He gestured again to the large man behind him, and I nearly pissed myself right there on the doorstep as the giant slowly withdrew a large handgun from his black jacket. I'm English, don't forget, and not only do we never see guns of any kind, but this was the *Midlands.* We didn't even really have gangs in the urban areas, and here I was growing up on a bloody farm, and suddenly a large hand cannon was being waved inches from my face.

And then the large man ejected the magazine and handed the now useless weapon to me.

It was, in many ways, a pointless gesture. Given his size alone, the best I could have done would have been to bloody his lip – although I can promise you I would have at least gone down fighting - and that was before he used any of his no doubt formidable "certain skills" on me. So him being unarmed wasn't actually reassuring... and yet, somehow, it was. It did at least make me feel, though my heart was pounding and I felt like I was having a nightmare, that they meant it. They weren't going to do anything to *me.*

But the girls. They'll do something to them.

It might not be the MacArthur girls. You don't know.

15

It might not be. This could all be a lie, a hidden camera show...

But it wasn't. I knew it wasn't. And even if it *wasn't* the MacArthur girls, one of those young women was going to be killed.

This is a dream. So just talk to them. Just talk to them, and you'll wake up later.

And then, crazily:

I wish Mum and Dad were here to fix this.

But they weren't.

In a stumbling sweep, I pretty much fell back against the hallway wall as I gestured for my two strange visitors to enter.

"Ok, great," said the Man in White, clapping his hands together, delightedly, and crossing the threshold. His large associate followed, his bulk sailing past me like a glacier, impossibly large in the tiny cottage hallway. I found myself suddenly thinking of what they said about vampires: you are powerless against them once you invite them into your home. The normal, so-familiar and sane sight of the courtyard outside disappeared behind the coffin lid of the front door as I pushed it closed.

***

"Ok if I sit down, Chris?" the Man in White said, already pulling out a chair from the kitchen table and sitting down in it. His large associate stood in the corner, hands crossed in front of his groin, one still holding the iPad. I nodded, thinking *I just need to hear them out, that's all,* and wildly wondering if I should offer them some tea. The Man in White's bright suit was just as stark against the terracotta floor and wall tiles of the old kitchen as his associate's had been against the snowy courtyard. For the said associate's part, his size was accentuated by the room, dark ceiling beams nearly brushing against his head. The de-fanged gun they'd given me was now lying on the kitchen counter, a grim reminder of the seriousness of the situation.

"You said... I just had to hear you out," I said quietly, the image of the kneeling and bound girls flashing before my eyes. Already, it didn't seem real. I leaned on the opposite wall from where the Man in White was sitting, not wanting to be within touching distance of such madness. "I'm listening, let's, let's, let's get on with this."

"That's fine, that's fine," the Man in White said, shrugging. "You've done a brave thing, Chris, letting us in like this. That took guts. You don't know us from Adam, right? And he's scary-looking, let's face it. *I* wouldn't let him in!" He chuckled at this last part, looking at his companion, who didn't return the glance and instead stared out of the kitchen window. "Big fella like that, turning up first thing in the morning... no, thank you."

The Man in White turned that sickening smile back to me and raised a finger in my direction. "*Guts.* That's going to be important from here on out. We'll talk about that shortly. First, we have a little multiple choice thing for you to do here, Chris, to make doubly sure you're the right person for the task, but I already think you're the man for the job. The boss has picked well." He leaned backwards and gestured at Black Suit again, who reached into his inner pocket and pulled out an envelope. He leaned forward and passed it to the Man in White; I noticed that he didn't need to step forward to do so. His reach was long enough, leaning, to pass the envelope across the room. The Man in White took it without a word and placed it on the table, sliding it in my direction.

"Just a personality test thing," he said. "Take a look."

"Hang on," I said, looking at the envelope like it was a bomb, "you didn't say anything about a test. You said I just had to hear you out."

"Yes, I did, and this is part of hearing us out," said the Man in White with a light sigh, as if I was being difficult. "You fill that in, then we explain. Look, the quicker it's done, the quicker we're out of your hair, right? And I'm sure you want that as much as I do."

"What else?" I suddenly snapped. "What else is there? You're already adding things. Just tell me what else you've got, you're not being fair." I was angry, but it was coming out like the words of a child. I couldn't shift the idea of my Mum coming home and seeing these two in *her* kitchen, total reality meeting insanity. But that wouldn't happen because—

They knew. They knew your parents are away for two weeks. That's why they've come now.

That immediately killed any fire I had stone dead. I reminded myself to be very, very careful, however familiar and ordinary my surroundings.

"Hey, you know what, I apologise," the Man in White said, suddenly throwing up his hands and leaning forward slightly in his seat, sighing once more. "It's been... it's been a hell of a week, and I was up late. We came here early because we wanted to make sure you were in, blah blah blah... I'm being snappy. My apologies."

For a moment, I didn't know what to say. I was thrown anew by this shift in demeanour. Then:

"Why me? Why have you, I mean, why *me*?" I asked.

"Ah, I'll be honest, Chris," the Man in White said, scratching at his cheek and looking out the window, "I'd like to say that it's because you're special, but y'know, it's not. Quite the opposite in fact. It's what my employer wanted. A regular guy. Young. Where do you work, Chris?"

You already know, I thought. But instead, I said,

"Ventures. The call centre."

"Mm-hmm. And what do you plan to do after that?"

"I don't know." I could feel myself reddening slightly, and I was getting angrier.

"No plans?"

"*No.* And don't take the piss," I said, but not as strongly as I'd like. My fingers were working around themselves nervously. The Man in White smirked.

"Open the envelope, Chris."

That was when something hit me. The white suit he was wearing *wasn't* just a fashion choice. I mean, who actually dresses like that? Nobody, at least nobody in reality. Yeah, ok, his big friend was in standard spook/secret service/bodyguard gear, but this guy? He was a walking cliché. It was like somebody had said to me, *Hey Chris, can you imagine a Colombian drug lord for me please?* And this guy had popped up as the end result. The question was... why? I didn't think this was all a wind-up – the video feed had been too damn real, and I can't imagine any person I knew capable of such cruel humor or any TV show that would be allowed to get away with such material – but who was he trying to fool? Or intimidate? Or convince?

I caught myself, seeing a slight furrow in the Man in White's brow due to my silence, but I tried to make a mental note of what I'd realized. Maybe nothing, maybe something, but I hadn't *completely* lost my nerve, it seemed. I moved forward and gingerly picked up the envelope.

"It's just a test, nothing to worry about," the Man said, leaning back in his chair and lacing his fingers together. With a fresh perspective, I realized that all he was missing was a fluffy white cat to stroke. "Hey, you might even enjoy it. You know, like those quizzes in magazines? That kind of thing." I opened the envelope as he spoke and saw exactly what he'd described: three sheets of A4 paper covered in questions and multiple choice tick boxes. I looked at the paper and looked back at his smiling face. "Should take about 15 minutes," he said. I looked at the hulk in the corner.

"You've done this too, I assume?" I asked. I felt light-headed. To my surprise, the big man shook his head slowly in response.

"Take a seat, Chris," the Man in White said, gesturing to one of the chairs.

"I don't need your permission," I said, feeling my skin burn. The Man in White grinned wider and turned to the large man with a *get-a-load-of-this-guy* look. The big man's face seemed expressionless, but the mouth *might* have twitched a little.

"Guts, yes sir, guts," the Man in White said. "Ok, apologies, your house. Well, not your house, your parents', but hey. Take your time with that anyway. But the sooner it's done, the sooner we're out of here, which, you know, we could do right now if you want, but... you know."

"I know. Let me concentrate," I said, taking a pen out of the drawer and sitting down.

"Sure thing, Chris," he said. I began the test.

I was surprised by how normal it was. *I am someone who is confident at making decisions: Strongly agree, somewhat agree, not sure, somewhat disagree, strongly disagree. I have a strong sense of right and wrong. I am someone who thinks about the consequences*

21

of my actions. On and on it went. It took longer than fifteen minutes, I think. Even then, I didn't want to half-ass a personality test. In hindsight, people would probably have said to me that I should have lied. I thought about it, sure, but I didn't know if I would be making things better or worse. You could only say I should have lied with the gift of *hindsight.* I didn't have that gift at the time.

Eventually, I finished and handed it back to the white-suited man, who by now was fiddling with his phone. He looked up, grinned, took it from me, and then went through it, marking something into his phone as he went through each question. I watched in silence, looking at the large man on the opposite side of the room out of the corner of my eye.

"Okaaaaay, Chris," the Man in White said, putting his phone in his pocket and looking up. "Good, that all looks good. Great, in fact."

I didn't want to know what that meant. I felt a heavy sensation in my stomach and knew that this was the beginning of the rabbit hole. There was a noose tightening around my neck, and even though I knew I could stop it... I couldn't. In fact, it *wasn't* tightening, was it? It was already tight. I was trapped from the moment I opened the door; from the moment I'd heard a word he said. I didn't *have* a choice. Not really.

"Here's the situation, Chris," the Man in White said, standing slightly to draw his chair nearer to mine and then sitting with his forearms on his thighs. "You have a chance, right now, today, to be a hero. A real, honest-to-goodness hero. Sound good?"

I didn't respond.

"You, *you* Chris," the Man in White said, grinning like a game show host from hell and pointing at me once more, "can save all of those girls' lives. Every single one of them. Do you know how few people get to do something like that? To actually be a hero? Well, today you do. Or tomorrow. However long you like, but I probably wouldn't leave it too long if I were you."

"Leave *what* too long?" I said, realizing my arms were trembling as I continued to sit. The Man in White sat back and grinned, savouring the moment.

"You have to kill someone, Chris," the Man in White said, as theatrically as possible. His voice lowered an octave as he spoke. If it wasn't for the horror of what he'd said, I would have laughed. "Anyone you like. Or dislike, I suppose. *Some*one, is the point. You have to murder another human being within the next thirteen days, starting today. Well, by 3 pm on the thirteenth day, to be precise."

I couldn't speak. The Man in White took my silence as understanding and continued.

"The simplest way of explaining it is to tell you how the time limits work," he said. "Don't blame me. I didn't think up the timing; that's down to the boss. It's a little unfair because if you agree to all this, the first window of time already started at 6 am this morning. So you're a little behind. But that's how it works: 6 am to 3 pm, 3 pm to midnight, and then the next countdown starts at 6 am the following morning. Each segment, if you like, is therefore nine hours long. With me?"

I actually nodded, stunned.

"Ok," he continued, "so, case in point, if you take on the challenge, as it were, and you haven't killed anyone by 3 pm today, we start with Olivia – oldest to youngest we go – and we cut off her right arm. If you haven't killed anyone by midnight *tonight,* it's her left arm. Then, if you don't kill anyone between 6 am and 3 pm tomorrow, it's her right leg. At midnight, her left leg. And, as you can probably guess, the last thing to go - if the job isn't done inside the *next* block of time after *that* – will be her head. Then it's the next girl and so on and so on until either you get the job done or, well... we run out of girls."

I stared at him. And stared at him. And at the man in the corner. And back at the Man in White. The suit, what he was saying... it wasn't real. *He* wasn't real. And all I could ask was:

"W*hy?*" My voice was high and breathy.

To my complete lack of surprise, the Man in White shrugged in response.

"I have *no* idea, Chris, I really don't," the Man in White said, sighing again. "Rich people... they're fucked in the head. They get a kick out of this kind of thing. Anyway, there are some rules involved, so I have to go through them before you make any kind

24

of decision, all right? The boss wants to make sure you're, y'know, fully informed. But listen carefully, as then it's going to be decision time, and we need an answer quickly. Okay?"

"... but ..."

"Okay, number one: you have to live a normal life while this is going on," the Man in White said, ignoring my question and holding up a finger to note the rule number. "No fun in making a normal man into a killer without him being normal, in the boss's eyes. So you can't, y'know, quit work and then just go nuts. All right? You have to live a normal life and be a killer as a normal man. And we know you've used up all of your days off at work. In fact, if you take on the task and you're late for work any of the days that you're supposed to be in, one of the girls dies each time. Understand?"

Again, I just looked at him.

"Number two, and I think this goes without saying, you can't go to the police if you agree to take us up on this," he continued. "I mean, as I say, if you go to them now you'll get nowhere. Trust me. And I'm sure you're already thinking *how would we know*, but, as I'll explain in a bit, we won't even *have* to know that you've actually gone to the police. If at any point we don't know what you're doing, they die. *All* of them. I'll explain how you'll be monitored for the thirteen days if you agree, but for now, you just need to know that if you begin this, going to the police is *not* an option if you want the girls to live."

"Number three: just as with this morning, *any* time you want to quit, you can quit. It's totally up to you. But bear in mind that, as you can probably guess, the girls die in the manner previously described. That's not really a rule as such, but you need to know this fact."

I was already aware of the argument in my head, albeit very distantly. One voice talking:

I can't kill anyone, I won't kill anyone, the idea is just.... just....

And the other voice in response, too clear and big to avoid, yet too much to understand:

Then five girls will die in great pain if you don't.

"Number four," the Man in White continued, furrowing his brow for a moment as he tried to recall what came next, "... no guns, no explosives. Perhaps a bit pointless that one, as I know you can't get any of the former and have no idea how to make the latter, but still, it has to be said. The boss considers that cheating. And no poisons, no running someone over. It has to be up close and personal."

I thought of the girls in the room, as part of my brain already whispered *what about Steve at the call centre? He's cheating on his wife and starts fights on nights out. He's not a good guy. He's someone who—*

I almost slapped myself to end that thinking, right then and there.

Listen: there are no words to describe the unreality of the situation, so I'm going to stop trying to find them as I'll just be repeating myself. Take it from me: I could not believe this was happening. Just assume that from here on in. I don't like to revisit any of this too much as it is.

"Number five: this one is important. You are limited in your selection of victims. No suicidal people, no one with a terminal illness, and no one at death's door. They have to *want* to live. That's the whole point. They have to be under sixty-five years old. Yeah, I know, they could live to a hundred or something, right? Well, that's why that age is the cut off. They have to be young enough to have a good amount of life left, at least a decade or two. No one brain dead in, like, a coma or something. No vegetables. We'll know who you kill, so it will be very easy for us to go through the details of your victim, and we *will* wait to release the girls... but we'll stop the cutting clock. Basically, for this rule, remember this: have to be healthy, want to live, be under sixty-five, and otherwise under no threat of dying anytime soon.

"Number six: again, not really a rule, but something you need to know: evidence," the man said. "*You* don't have to worry about it. *We* worry about that. We can clean a room, we can get to the right people, we can make evidence disappear. You don't have to worry about the law, Chris... unless someone sees you do it. Then you're writing someone *else's* death sentence, as they will need to be silenced. You with me? But mainly, you only have to worry about having the courage to do the deed." The Man in White leant back in his chair again, not taking his eyes off me.

"Annnd those are all the rules, really," he said lacing his fingers over his stomach. There was silence. I thought I was going to faint.

"How... how will you..."

"The *details* of how we're going to run it can wait, Chris," the Man in White said, forming a pinching shape with his thumb and forefinger on *details.* "You know the rules now. Everything we've said, you can trust, and I can prove it. I just need to know your decision in *principle* now, Chris. Being honest with you, the sooner I can start the clock ticking, the better. Are you doing this?"

"I ..."

They're going to die? They're going to die? All of them? Unless I—

"Chris?"

"I mean... are you kidding? You can't just, you can't, you can't just sit there and—"

"I get it Chris, and look, this isn't the first time we've done this either. We'll come to that shortly, but I know how to expedite a decision," the Man in White said, "because hey, how can you know how far you can go unless, you know... you know? You know what I mean. Ugh, look, it's early and I'm talking crap. Let me simplify it. I'm going to help you make up your mind."

I froze at first and then was about to leap out of the chair and bolt for the door, promises or no promises, but the Man in White barked a short laugh that confused me enough to make me pause.

"Not like that!" he chuckled, waving a hand, "We promised, didn't we? You'll learn that we keep our promises. *We're not going to hurt you or anyone you love,* Chris. This is just to help get things moving one way or another." He drew another phone from another pocket – a smaller, older, more basic model – and dialed a number. He didn't put it to his ear. He saw me and held up a finger – *one moment* – and waited for a connection on the other end. Once he got it, he placed the phone on the table, face up.

"Oooookay, the decision clock is now ticking," he said. "In one minute's time, Olivia—she's the oldest by a few minutes, as you may know—loses a finger. One minute after *that,* she loses the next, and so on, until she runs out of digits, then we begin on the rest of her in the order previously described, and then on to the next of her sisters. That'll be the next oldest, so... Mary? I want to say, Mary?" The Man in White asked, turning to his companion as if trying to remember who scored the winner at United on Saturday. The large man in the corner nodded without speaking. "Mm, Mary then. And then we work our way through the others in the same way. If it's going to be a no from you Chris, speaking as an objective observer here, I'd spit that out sooner rather than later and save those girls a lot of pain."

"What?" I screamed, jumping up from my chair. "You said I only had to hear you out and no one would die! What is this?!"

"No, I said if you *didn't* hear us out someone *would* die," the Man in White said patiently. "You've now heard us out. Thank you. The *next* part—now—is decision time. See? But what you say *is* binding. Let me make it clear: if you say no, the girls will die in the pretty damn unpleasant way I already described, plus the fingers and toes thing. Got it? If you say *yes,* the Process starts, and you have the chance to save them. You *can* still quit at any time, but quitting means they die. Got it?" He suddenly shook his hands in the air, mildly frustrated with himself.

"Okay, okay, listen, it's this simple. If you say no now, the girls die, very slowly and very painfully. If you say yes, you *do* have to kill someone, but that will save all the girls only if you get it done soon enough. Say yes and then back out: they all die. Say yes and take too long: they lose limbs and heads at preset intervals until there are no girls left or until you finally kill someone. Okay? So what's it going to be?"

The sense of pressure, of time being just unstoppable, vital, and terrifying thundered through my veins.

"Wait, *stop!*" I screamed, pulling impotently at my hair. "I can't kill anybody, stop, stop *cutting* her, what, are you doing that now? *Are you cutting her finger now?*"

"In about... twelve seconds, yes," the Man in White said, looking at the phone screen. "What's your answer?"

It couldn't be true. There was no way they were cutting off a girl's finger. It had to be a wind-up. But it didn't *feel* like a wind-up, who would *do* such a wind-up, cutting a girl's finger time murder what what *what*—

"Chris?" the Man in White asked when he'd received nothing but silence. "What do you—oh, there's a minute. Ok, they'll be cutting the finger off now."

"*I told you to wait!*" I screamed, and darted forward to grab the phone, but without even seeming to move the large man was suddenly there, my wrist in his huge hand and he was doing something to it, something that didn't seem to actually hurt that much yet it made my arm go numb and dropped me to my knees hard enough for one of them to bang painfully on the kitchen tiles. He released me almost immediately, but he remained by the table standing over me. I held my wrist tightly and looked up at them both from the floor.

"Can't do that, Chris," the Man in White said, apologetically. "We're not messing with *your* stuff, and we've been nothing but respectful to you. Sorry about that, but you know, you shouldn't touch other people's things. Forty seconds until the next finger."

"*Stop it!*" I screamed, but the Man in White just shrugged. *I already told you.*

"I can't Chris, not without an answer," he said, sighing, but it wasn't sarcastic. The sigh was sincere; I'm sure of it. "It's a tough one though. I do understand that. Uh..."—he leaned over slightly to check— "... twenty seconds."

"Please! Tell them to stop! How do I even know you're really doing it?" I screamed, scrambling to my feet. Even as I was screaming, I was doubting. After all, this was something out of a film, and it was difficult to believe they really *were* cutting off a girl's fingers... but the *panic* I felt at that moment, the terror....

"They wouldn't listen to me, Chris. They've been told only to respond to one of two answers. And as for how do you know, well my employer has instructed me to show you *after* your decision. I think he sees it as a test of faith kind of thing. Seriously, you only have a few more seconds until the next one goes."

All I could think was:

Five of them being slowly cut into pieces is worse than one person *dying. It just makes sense. You can't let them die like that, Chris.*

But I also knew that I couldn't kill anyone... just like I thought, deep down, that I *could.*

Could I do it if I picked someone bad? Someone who deserved it?

"Okay, the second finger will be going now—"

"I'll do it!" I screamed, *"Don't cut off the other finger. I'll do it!"*

To this day, I carry the guilt of knowing that I'd already decided—through logic alone—that I was going to do it, even before they'd cut Olivia's *first* finger off. I'd made my choice and couldn't admit it to myself. The guilt of delay. The guilt of procrastination. The guilt of knowing that the only thing that put that girl through the terrible pain of having two fingers sliced off was my lack of ability to admit that which I already knew.

The Man in White didn't respond and instead picked up the phone and put it to his ear.

"Have you done the second finger yet?" he asked. There was a pause while he waited for an answer. "Okay, thought so. Bye." He put the phone down and looked at me again. "Yeah, he hasn't done it yet, but because the second minute marker was passed, he's got to cut it off anyway. He's working under the rules, just like me."

"*Stop him!*" I screeched, but I knew it was pointless. The rules. Already, it seemed, I was working under them too. "*I won't do it. I'll back out!*"

"That's totally up to you Chris, totally up to you, but you've already said yes, I'm afraid," the Man in White said as he slid the small phone back into his pocket. "That means if you back out... well, you know. At least they won't go through the whole fingers and toes thing, just the arms and legs and head thing. A quicker death. But death for all of them nevertheless. Are you backing out?"

I was in, I was *in,* and there was only one way out. Well, two ways, but one I couldn't ever live with and one that I just wasn't sure I could actually carry out.

But I would have to, wouldn't I? I would have to. At least, that's how I saw it. You may see it differently, but you weren't there, you weren't me, so fuck you.

"Chris?"

All I could do was shake my head. The big man raised the iPad once more and passed it to the Man in White.

"Okaaaaay," said the Man in White absently, looking from me to the actual clock on the farmhouse wall to make a mental note of the time. "You wanted proof as well, didn't you?" he asked, tapping at the tablet that was now in his hand. "Ok, take a look aaaaat... this," he said, turning it around to show me the screen.

The sound was off, but the image before me was the face of Olivia MacArthur. I recognized her easily without her blindfold on. She'd done enough magazine covers and even a few product endorsements in the past, so I knew her straight away, despite the dirt and tear tracks and contorted expression that was plastered onto her screaming face. I lunged forward to grab the iPad, not thinking, but the Man in White pulled it out of reach as his companion grabbed my shoulder, holding me in place. I struck at the big man's arm, not looking at him as I screamed at the Man in White, but it seemed to have no effect. As for White, he actually looked shocked.

"Stop it, Chris," he said, holding the tablet to his chest. He wasn't being sarcastic either. "Calm down. That's not helping anything."

"Why are you doing this? Why? What's wrong with you? Who are you working for?" I barked, slowing my struggles and holding up my hands, pleading for sanity. In response, the Man in White brought up the onscreen interface again and the sound broke in. Sobs and cries intensified as two hands grabbed Olivia's shoulders and her wrist was grabbed and slowly raised by a third assailant's grip, revealing the freshly sawn-off and cauterized stumps of her index and middle fingers.

"Did you get that?" the Man in White asked, his voice slightly raised enough so that I knew he wasn't speaking to me. There was a pause and then the sound of rustling paper. Even in her pain, Olivia looked confused, looking at someone off-screen, and then frantically nodded, agreeing desperately to avoid retribution.

"Why... a-are you doing this?" she asked, her voice barely sounding human through her sobbing and the hoarseness in her throat... yet *robotic*, as if she were reciting someone else's words, which was, of course, exactly what she was doing. "Why... wh-what's wrong with you ... wh-who are you working for..."

My words from seconds ago. Written down and shown to her to read aloud to prove once again beyond any doubt that this was live. And real. The Man in White nodded, seeing my comprehension. The screen was locked again; the iPad was placed upon the table.

"Okay," he said, cautiously, as if waiting for me to try and pounce again. "The clock is ticking. Sorry to take up any of that time now, but I need to make sure we have a moment to answer any more questions you might have and to go over a few logistical details, particularly the ones involving my friend here. You're going to be seeing quite a bit of him."

"You don't have to do this," I begged. "You can change your mind. You can stop this. You don't have to do this. You don't have to make *me* do this. Please stop."

"Sorry, Chris. I really understand you saying that, but it's just not an option here. Better not to waste time now mate, seriously." He pointed at the chair. "Sit down, try and slow your breathing and relax a bit more, and I'll run through a few last bits of info. Then I can be on my way and leave you to it. Now I'm going to give you something to bear in mind while we're talking to try and help get the ball rolling, so to speak. To, you know, save you and the girls as much time as possible, because as you've seen, we go to the *minute* on this. You see it doesn't matter if you've got someone by the throat and start squeezing at, say, 2:59 pm. If they're still alive by 3:00 pm, or whenever that particular time deadline is, that's a limb or a head coming off. Do you see?"

I saw. And even as the room spun and I felt like I was going to faint, he asked his next question and I realized that he hadn't needed to; that I was already—in a distant part of my mind—*asking it myself:*

"So as I say, try and be thinking as we're talking. Is there anyone you know, perhaps, that you believe you could kill?

Anyone that—given that you *have* to kill *someone*—is bad *enough* that they deserve to die more than an innocent? Anyone that deserves to die more than these girls who do so much charity work for others? Your victim doesn't have to be a pedophile or a rapist or whatever, just someone that you think deserves it more than the girls. Anyone who is, quite frankly, just a bastard or a bitch."

He shrugged.

"Chris? Do you know anyone like that?"

***

Chapter Two: Previous Candidates, The Selection Process Begins, and Bypassing The Gatekeeper

***

I want you to know something from here on out. Hindsight is a wonderful, blissful, unrealistic idiot. That's the one good thing to come out of all of this. I learned to be easier on myself when I can't think of things to do or say "at the time." The Process taught me that much.

Can you imagine? Looking back on all that happened and picking apart Every. Single. Decision. Was this right; could I have done that; *should* I have done that; *oh my God, why didn't I think of that...*

All the time. Every day. All the counselors in the world couldn't help because I could never tell them what really happened, although I came close a few times. I think I've found a way to make it better, though. I think so. A way to find peace of a sort.

But I still have to get the story out of me.

Anyway, the point I'm trying to make is this: while I have no intention of ever letting this account be read by anyone for as long as I live, it may still be found when I'm dead. If it is, then I need to make something very clear indeed.

You shouldn't judge my choices. I'm not you, and more importantly, you sure as hell weren't me *at that time.* The knowledge that in a few hours a young woman is going to lose another limb, or her *life*, because of your choices... that tends to have a *tremendous* impact on your higher reasoning. So save me the *I would have done this, why didn't you do this* bullshit. I can guarantee that *after the fact* I've thought about whatever approach you've come up with, because I've had the misfortune of going through them *all* in my head over the last nine years. Non-stop. "At the time" makes all the difference. "At the time" I was a fucking idiot.

It was just me. On my own. A stupid punk kid. And the clock. Always the clock.

Well... just me and Klaus.

***

"Oh, wait, that reminds me," the Man in White said, clicking his fingers and then pointing them at the huge man who was now standing behind me. "What do you want to call him?"

"What?" I asked. I was pretty numb now. It was a blessing.

"My friend here," the Man in White said. "He's going to be with you pretty much constantly until this ends, one way or the other, so you need to decide what to call him." The question was ludicrous, as if we were talking about a dog.

"Doesn't... he have a name?"

"Of course he does, but *you* don't get to know that. I could have made one up, but I always prefer to let you guys decide it for yourselves. I could tell you that I do that because it'll help you remember, but really it's because it's just one of those things that makes a job interesting, you know? So. What name?"

I turned slightly, not wanting to stare at the large man. He'd stepped back, not to give me a better look—Klaus isn't that kind of guy—but because he'd moved naturally into a more relaxed position (or whatever he considered relaxed) and now I could see and consider him clearly. As crazy and strangely lighthearted as the question seemed in that situation, my mind had already told me the answer. It had already seen the blonde hair, the over-the-top government spook get-up, the ridiculously Aryan *look* of the guy, and had come up with an answer.

"Klaus," I said, quietly.

"Klaus? Like a German guy?" the Man in White cried and clapped his hands together once as he laughed. "Ha! That's a new one! You hear that, *Klausy?*" His finger wagged in the large man's direction, who from that moment and forevermore would be Klaus in my eyes. Klaus, for his part, didn't change his position or facial expression in the slightest. He simply continued to loom. And then something hit me.

"A new... wait, you like to let 'us guys' decide it for ourselves?" I asked, almost reluctant to point out what I'd noticed

41

in case it was a big slip up on his part, one that could get me in trouble because I shouldn't know... but I *had* to know. "This isn't the first time you've done this. Or something like this. Is it?"

"Oh, no, no," said White, speaking in a slightly surprised tone of voice that immediately told me it wasn't a slip up at all. "Didn't I tell you? Oh, no, wait, I didn't, did I? I didn't show you the video or anything. Hold on," he said, holding up a gloved finger as he picked up the iPad from the table again and began to poke at it. "Fancy gloves," he said offhandedly as he tapped away. "You can get similar ones at the petrol station, you know, crappy woolen ones, but these are fancy. They still look nice and you can't even notice they have the special tips that let you use a touchscreen. Pretty cool. You should get some; they still aren't really *that* much. They don't work with the thumbprint lock though. You have to take them off for that."

He talked as if he were on a sales call, and I wanted to kill him.

You could kill him. That would count.

And Klaus would kill me *before I even picked up a knife.*

"Here, here," White said eagerly, turning the pad around once more. "Some more people you might recognize. Don't worry. This isn't, you know ...live footage or whatever. It's recorded. It's not nice though. See him? You recognize him?"

I did. I recognized the man onscreen immediately and any hope that might have remained – impotent, desperate hope that still clung to this being bullshit or a sick prank or *something* – disappeared.

Onscreen, I saw some slightly shaky but otherwise clear footage of Peter Carsdale, who had briefly been a news item about two years prior. The only reason I remembered him was because of the angle behind the story and because he was a West Midlands guy. He'd been quite sensationally found innocent during his trial for the murder of Priesh Kamani due to a cast-iron alibi turning up halfway through the trial. Prior to that, it looked like an open-and-shut case of murder to the local media, which had already been baying for his blood (at least as much as mere *local* media can actually bay). Once his guilt was in doubt, it was a *national* media item for about a day before being replaced by whatever bullshit a Kardashian was up to at the time. I remembered them finding him innocent very clearly. I'd been really pleased. I like a comeback story. I always have.

I watched as Peter Carsdale beat Priesh Kamani to death with a crowbar before my eyes. I *assumed* it was Priesh Kamani. It was clearly an Indian man, but the flying hands and shaky camera and blood and distorted features made it difficult to tell.

Clearly, this was footage that didn't make it to trial.

It was dark wherever they were. Outside at night, perhaps. The ground beneath the stricken Kamani was concrete, so it was doubtful that they were indoors. I wanted to look away, but I didn't. A man was dying before my eyes. It was captivating, and I couldn't help it. It would have made me feel sick normally, but I didn't think I could feel any more nauseated than I already did.

"And this one," White said, flicking the image sideways to reveal the frozen first frame of another video, this one better lit. He pressed play. The video showed a cheap hotel room where a struggling, bound, and gagged middle-aged woman thrashed against the bonds tying her to the bed... and against the light weight of the thin, much younger woman that sat astride her waist. The younger woman was weeping and held a kitchen knife in her trembling hand. I didn't recognize either of them.

"Don't make me do this," she sobbed, turning and looking to someone off-camera. "Please. Don't make me do this." The response that came was quiet and muffled and obviously not the voice of whoever was holding the camera, as it seemed to come from a man standing some distance from the microphone. I could still hear him, though. I wish I hadn't. The words were so horribly prophetic.

"You don't have to," the speaker said, calmly. "We're not making you do anything. This is your choice."

In response, the young woman's head fell backwards as she screamed, and her hand gripped the knife's handle tightly. She then moved lightning-fast. Suddenly, the knife shot up and over and *down*, again and again and again in a frenzied blur as it plunged into the older woman's throat and chest. Her victim's struggles ceased after the second strike, but the younger woman kept going, screaming all the while as blood flecked her arms and chest.

The screen went black once more.

"Recognise any of those people?" White asked, laying the tablet down.

"The first one," I mumbled.

"Sorry?" White asked, his forehead creasing as he sat forward slightly.

"The first one," I repeated, more loudly.

"Oh, not the second as well?" White said, sounding genuinely surprised. "That was Jenny Tuttle. Recognise the name?" I did, vaguely, once I'd heard it. That name had been in the news, but I recalled it being mentioned in a rape case. Obviously, that was wrong.

"Yes. Vaguely. That's older than the Peter Carsdale case, isn't it?"

"That's right. Two years before. We don't film them anymore like *this*. Logistically, it makes things more difficult. We have to have somebody with a decent camera there, and we prefer, uh, *Klaus* to keep his hands free. You *will* have a camera feed on you at all times, but it doesn't give us as good a picture as this, so we don't make such a big deal of actually recording and storing it. We don't *need* to anymore, really. We have enough footage to make our point to the new guys."

I'm going to have a camera feed on me at all times. "How do you mean", was going to be the next question past my lips, but the usual mental hierarchy of importance came into play as that thought was kicked aside by:

"What point? What point are you trying to make?"

"That you don't have to worry about us fucking you, Chris. You don't remember the Tuttle case very well, but you can look it up. Just like the Carsdale case, she ended up with a watertight alibi that saved her behind, one that came out of nowhere. We *could* have let her hang. Peter too, but we didn't. We were as good as our word, and *these are the cases that actually made it to court.* That doesn't happen, normally. We've done this lots of times Chris, and on the rare instances where our Participant got into legal trouble—"

"Your what?"

"Our Participant, that's what you are now. On the instances where our Participant was caught, we got them off, as promised. The boss is very, very big on *rules,* Chris, as you've probably realized, but that means we have to abide by them too. Whatever we say we'll do, we'll do, so keep up *your* end of the bargain, and we'll keep up *ours.*"

Silence.

"But what's the *point* of this?" I asked again, lost for anything else to say. White shrugged, again, and I wanted to kill him, just like that.

"I told you. It's not my job to know, Chris. I just have to pass the information on to you. Oh, and this as well. *Klaus?*" White said, chuckling as he used the name, and turned in his seat, holding out a hand to his associate. Klaus reached a gloved hand inside his jacket and pulled something black out of his inside pocket. It looked like an activity monitor or something, attached to a small strap. He handed it to the Man in White.

"You have to attach this to your ankle," White said, giving it to me. "As you can probably guess, it's a tag. Once it's on, you won't be able to take it off unless you cut it off, or we do so using the correct device. Obviously, if the former happens, the girls die, yadda yadda yadda. This will let us know where you are, and when, but to be honest, this is really just added insurance, and enables us to track you around the building at work. Or at least we will if this lasts until Monday and you do actually have to go into work. You know, because it might raise a few eyebrows if Klausy here rocks up and sits next to you in your cubicle."

"Wait," I said, another sinking feeling beginning in my stomach as I held the black lump of plastic in my hand. I could only assume that, by this point, my stomach had sunk to somewhere around my ankles. "What do you mean? Why would Klaus even be there even if, even if, you know, people at work wouldn't, uh, look what the fuck are you talking about?" I thought I knew what he meant and the idea of it was making me babble.

"Well... obviously..." said White, looking so genuinely confused that he even briefly glanced at Klaus for confirmation that it *was* obvious, "you'll have a chaperone. How else would we make totally sure you weren't up to anything? We have a wire for you to wear at all times, and you will also be wearing a camera pin for the feed—Klaus will have spare batteries for you to replace at set intervals so they don't run out, no excuses—but wherever you are, he'll be close by. How did you *think* we are going to be totally sure? Oh no. When I leave today, Klaus stays here with you. He goes where you go, and when you're at work, he'll be outside in the car park, monitoring your feeds. If those feeds go dead, blah blah blah, you know. They won't. These are *extremely* expensive and state of the art. There's only one way they're going dead, and that's if someone messes with them." He pointed at me and smiled in a way that was almost apologetic.

"No. No," I babbled, not knowing why I was freaking out so much at this—I'd just agreed to commit murder, after all—but I was. I didn't agree to all this extra stuff. "He can't stay here. My parents..." This man, this *thing,* being with me all the time? The thought was awful and worse was the one that came with it:

I'd better get this done quickly so that I can be rid of him.

I pushed it away, hard, but the realization that they were already changing me was sickening.

"Your parents are away for two weeks," White said. "And this will all be over one way or another, long before they get back." I pictured Mum and Dad walking in the door, happy and refreshed, unaware that their son had become a killer in their absence. Then the Man in White stood, and adrenalin shot through me once again as I realized that he was about to leave.

"That's it?" I shrieked, and lowered my voice when I spoke again. I'd noticed that Klaus had straightened up too. "You're leaving?"

"Nothing more to add really, Chris," the Man in White said, and in a bizarre moment, he extended his hand for me to shake. I didn't take it. I simply stood there trembling, with my mouth hanging open. "Klaus will tell me when you've done the job, and I'll stop the clock and run the usual checks. Then we'll be finished. If there's anything you think of in the meantime, just ask Klaus, and he'll ask me. But you'd probably be best just to get a move on." He paused, and his voice softened when he spoke again. "Look, you really *could* just quit right now, you know. You don't have to do anything. I know you think that's not a real option, but it is. Just say the word."

"Don't... don't..."

"Just... really. If you're going to actually *do* this... don't get any ideas," White said, ignoring me, but dropping his hand back to his side. "Not only for your own safety," he nodded in Klaus' direction, "but for, you know, theirs. Any hint of messing around, they're done. We'll do it in a heartbeat. We're monitoring your phone, laptop, and emails, too—if you think I'm bullshitting you, I can tell you that you were last on YouPorn on your laptop and Cracked.com on your phone, and the last email you sent was to GoDaddy customer support—plus, if any cops come for Klaus, not only will he deal with them *very* easily and you'll have *that* on your conscience, but the girls too. Hey, I don't wanna repeat myself, but I feel like I've gotta be clear. But look. It's up to you."

"But it isn't fair! If I have to go to work, then that's taking up time, isn't it?" I hissed, clutching at straws. "That's almost guaranteeing that on work days, the girls are getting... it's not fair! I can't kill someone while I'm working, can I?"

I will never forget his next words.

"Are you sure, Chris?" he said, his face blank and awful behind the dark mirrors of his sunglasses. I saw my own face reflecting back at me, slackening before my eyes. "There aren't CCTV cameras everywhere at your building. We checked. Isn't there *someone* at your workplace that is just an utter *cunt?*"

I just stood there, paralysed by both the reality of my situation and, God help me, the possibilities.

"I probably won't see you again, Chris," the Man in White said, "and for what it's worth, I *am* sorry. If it wasn't me telling you all this, it'd be someone else. Good luck. Remember: stay off camera and out of sight of witnesses, and it's almost certain that you won't even hear from the police. We'll take care of you either way."

He gave Klaus a thumbs up. Klaus nodded. Then the Man in White pointed at the emptied gun on the counter.

"I'm going to take that. It can't help you anyway, and y'know, we were just making a point." He picked the weapon up and stashed it inside his jacket, and then he walked out of the kitchen and into the hallway, heading for the front door. I stood frozen to the spot, wanting to scream something to make him wait, but the clock was already ticking. Stopping *him* would just be taking up valuable time.

Valuable time? Valuable time? You can't do this.

I wondered vaguely how they'd gotten here. Was there a car somewhere? It certainly wasn't outside in the courtyard. I could follow him to try and get the plates, but I knew Klaus would do something about that. I heard the front door open and close. The kitchen was then silent.

I didn't want to look at Klaus. I could feel his eyes drilling bloody holes in the back of my head. I thought about the Chris of an hour ago, lying in bed blissfully unaware. I wanted to be that guy so much that I hated him.

You have a job to do. The CLOCK. Is TICKING.

I knew it. I looked at the particular clock in my kitchen. To my surprise, it was already after nine thirty. The test must have taken longer than I thought. Klaus began to pull some cables out of his other jacket pocket, as well as a small microphone, two tiny battery packs, and something that looked like a pin badge. My wire and camera, by the looks of it.

"Can that wait a second? I need to do something first. I'm not going anywhere yet, so I won't need it, will I?" Klaus stopped moving, but continued staring at me. I took this as confirmation. Feeling like I would fall apart if I moved too quickly, I went to the drawer to get a pen and paper. I had to make a list. I needed criteria. This wasn't plain stalling, either; the *last* thing in the world I wanted to do was stall. I had just over five hours to choose, find, and kill another human being before Olivia lost the rest of her arm to go with her two already-missing fingers. If I could do that—save all five of them with only two fingers lost— then I would feel... I *thought* I would feel as if I could live with my actions. And if I was going to do that, then I needed to choose my target perfectly. The list was important. I needed to narrow this down from *everyone* to *someone*.

A list?! Are you cra—

I had to make a list.

"Sit down," I said to Klaus, without looking up. "You're making me uncomfortable."

As I stared at the sheet in front of me, I heard a scrape as the chair on the opposite side of the table was pulled out.

***

Half an hour later, I had barely written anything at all. I'd clarified nothing. Trying to disconnect my mind—to become as purely objective as possible, to remove emotion so that I could function—had helped a little but not enough. You might be thinking *the police, why didn't you try and call the police?* If you're thinking that, then you haven't been listening. At one point I got up to go for a piss, and Klaus followed me into the bathroom, standing behind me while I went. I wasn't getting away from him. I knew that the girls died if I really tried. And any more fucking around meant pissing away time as well as urine. There was only one way to go.

My "list" was useless. *Must deserve to die* wasn't very helpful, as that was obvious, but finding someone like that within the timescale I had? Not likely. The question was, I realized to my seemingly levelling-out horror, one of balance. Look at it this way:

Olivia and the girls were humanitarians. In my eyes, this made them "worth" more than, say, a rapist, or even just a straight-up asshole you might come across in the street. And let's say I took four Time Blocks (that was the way I thought about those 6 am to 3 pm and 3 pm to 12 am periods then, and the way I've thought about them ever since. I had to be scientific about it or I'd go insane) to really *really* drill it down and choose carefully. For example, say I used up all the time—the time it took for her to lose all of her limbs—making sure I was picking a total asshole, and then killed that someone before the fifth and final Block was up. The one that would mean her head and her life.

That would mean I'd have one dead asshole, but one humanitarian girl who was rendered a quadriplegic for the rest of her life. To me, that was *not* balance. *But...* then say I didn't choose quite as carefully, killed someone I thought was *probably* enough of an asshole within the *current* Time Block that I was in—i.e., I killed someone before 3 pm that first day—and Olivia lost no limbs at all. Could I live with knowing I rushed it? That *maybe* I wrong? That wouldn't work either. My decision, therefore, was this:

I could afford to go into the *third* Time Block. Olivia could afford to lose two arms, if that was the cost of making sure I had chosen correctly. That meant I had until 2:59 pm tomorrow to kill someone. That, to me, was fair.

Think differently? You would have planned something else? Hey, maybe your plan would have been better. But you weren't there, you weren't me, and that was the decision I made. If it makes you feel any better, I think about it constantly. All the time. All. The. Time. So you're probably right.

Here was the list I had:

1. Must deserve to die.
2. Must be an adult.

3. Must have committed a violent crime against another human being: rape, assault, murder, GBH, manslaughter.

That was it. That was all I had. I was trying to narrow it down *so much,* but I could think of nothing else and the clock was ticking. And number "1" up there was just fucking useless. It was so vague and arbitrary and open to interpretation that I decided to cross it off the list. I could have just gone for the *"dickhead enough to die"* option, sure, but I wanted to go bigger, have stronger reasons than *that.*

Must be an adult. Well, that was just fucking obvious.

Must have committed a violent crime against another human being.

Adult. Violent crime.

A penny dropped, and it was so obvious that I cried out and banged my fist on the table for not thinking of it sooner. Klaus didn't jump, of course, remaining as inexpressive as ever, but I realized his gaze hadn't moved from me the entire time that I'd been working on my list.

Child abusers. Child rapists. People that I could kill with a *lot* less doubt.

Statistics prove conclusively that most child abusers are victims of abuse themselves, a voice whispered in my head. I knew it was true, but if I let myself look for excuses, I could find one to avoid killing *anyone,* and the girls died. These guys were now top of the list.

The sex offender registry online. Finding someone would be easier than I thought. And then I could—

My stomach lurched as I thought of what "then I could" meant. I thought I had it, but blackness was creeping in at the edges of my vision and then the room was falling sideways. I remember Klaus' face, inexpressive behind his sunglasses, turning without alarm as his gaze followed me all the way to the floor.

My head hurt a bit when I came around. I must have hit it when I fell, but more annoying was the light stinging sensation on my cheek. As I opened my eyes, I cried out once more, this time in shock. Klaus' rock-like visage filled my vision, and the stinging sensation came again as he slapped my face.

"I'm awake!" I squeaked, and then I realized that I was in the living room, seated in one of the armchairs. Klaus must have moved me into a more supportive seat to bring me around. His meaty wrist came into view, poking out of the end of his sleeve, and I wondered what he was showing me. Klaus was communicating something? His gloved finger then came up, and moved the sleeve back further, revealing his gold watch. The finger then tapped the watch dial twice - sharply.

I was taken aback. He had, in a way, just done the girls a favour; if I'd stayed unconscious, that was more time wasted.

"Uh... thank you," I said, surprising myself. Klaus actually nodded in return and moved to the other side of the room to sit on the sofa. It creaked under his bulk as he sat, and his gaze once again settled on me from across the room. I felt my head where the pain seemed strongest. There was a small bump.

You fainted. Just thinking *about the prospect of actually* doing *it made you faint. What makes you think you can do this?*

My laptop—not this one, of course, this was bought solely for the purpose of writing this—was on the coffee table, the plumb centre of the living room. The low and slightly curved ceiling hung above ancient, thinning carpet. Mum thought it gave the place character.

Your parents—

I stood to retrieve the laptop, and that's when I realized something was taped to my chest. I looked down and saw a tiny microphone protruding from a thick strip of tape that wrapped around me twice. I felt a slight weight in my bathrobe pocket and plunged my hand into it. As I had thought, the microphone's battery pack was in there, along with another pack that presumably was connected to the pin-badge-looking camera that was stuck to the robe's lapel. Upon closer inspection, it really *was* disguised as a badge - a round, silver representation of the Union flag.

Klaus had done this while I was unconscious.

"You couldn't wait? I'm still in the fucking house!" I snapped. I wasn't scared of him. I wasn't breaking any rules, and I was pretty sure that he couldn't do anything to me unless I did something to him. And even *then* I just had to say that I quit, and he wouldn't do anything at all.

I assumed.

Klaus shrugged so subtly that I barely even saw it. There was a moment of angry silence, and I swore that I could hear the tape creaking slightly as I breathed rapidly in my impotent fury. Then I saw the clock. It was now past 10:30. The Man in White had left an hour ago! I decided to just fuck thoughts of Klaus off and get on with the task at hand. Still, I realized that he must have done this to my body while I was unconscious. He was as strong as he looked then.

"Don't do anything like that again," I muttered, a token resistance, and I didn't look at him for a response. I snatched my laptop off the table and opened it, sitting back down on the armchair as I did so. Klaus stood quickly and moved to sit on the chair's arm so that he could observe what was being done onscreen. I had to find some perverts, and quickly.

Easy, right? No.

The sex offender register - in the UK at least - doesn't work the way you might think. It isn't like Booking.com for sexual deviants, where you can tap in your location and it tells you how many rapists and child abusers are within a radius of your choosing. (*"There are THIRTY-SIX sexual predators nearby RIGHT NOW, and FORTY-TWO angry mob members currently viewing them in YOUR AREA. Hurry before the deviants are ALL KILLED!"*)

Unfortunately for me it was, and is, for running background checks on *specific individuals* near you, and for making sure that they aren't living near schools, et cetera. This means that you need to have someone in mind before you can make use of it; then you can run a search for *that specific person.* It makes sense, I suppose. It stops people from getting together on weekends at one of their buddies' houses with crates of beer, flaming torches, and baseball bats studded with nails before firing up the sex offender database and picking a victim at random for that evening's lynchin'; however, that meant it was of no use to me. I didn't know of anyone that I suspected of secretly being a sexual predator. The worst person I knew in that regard was my mate Pete, and he was at worst a bit grabby. Not at all socially acceptable I know, but not worthy of murder.

Try to think of famous cases. People have been in the news; people that got convicted for doing that kind of thing.

It was a nice idea, but a stupid one. Anyone I could think of in the news for being convicted *would be in jail.*

But what about older cases?

That was a good idea. It'd be easy to Google cases from ten years ago, and then it would just be a matter of finding out how long their sentences were and seeing if the perps were now out, right? No.

Even expanding my search out of the region and into the surrounding cities (I hadn't wanted to look too far afield as that meant extra driving time on top of potential locating time, potential lying-in-wait-all-day time... my hands were shaking as I typed), it turned out that, even in the rare instances where a sex offender's release from prison was reported, *the criminals in question didn't exactly set up a Facebook or Linkedin profile.* They moved away quietly and changed their names. Sure, the government and local authorities would keep tabs on them, but for the same friendly-lynch-mob reasons that the registry used, they didn't make those addresses and locations public. And even in the unlikely event that I *could* find one, I'd have to know his movements, wait for him to come home, catch him at the right time... all time-consuming and extremely difficult. I looked at the clock and realized that all this wasted searching had taken another half an hour. It was now gone eleven.

Less than four hours. Less than four hours and she loses an arm because an asshole didn't die.

What's next on the crime list? Murderers? You won't find any of them. Child abusers, rapists? You've just pretty much written that option off. Okay, so... violent people, drug dealers....

A light bulb went off in my head. Time-wise, it made total sense. It would be much easier for me to find a drug dealer than someone who had committed assault because I knew a few people who at least occasionally took drugs. No one hardcore, but they'd probably know people who *were*... and those people would know their dealers.

I didn't really know anyone who hung around with assault-y people, plus, someone who *did* like getting involved with violence would probably be reasonably good at it, better than me certainly. They might be more difficult to—

The world went grey again for a moment, but I slowed my breathing and brought myself back.

Rick. Rick knows a guy.

You're gonna kill Rick's friend?

Not his friend. His dealer.

I pictured the man, dressed in a pimp suit and smoking a crack pipe. Picturing lives that he'd ruined by peddling his poison. I pictured myself killing someone like that.

It can't just be weed or speed. It's got to be the harder stuff. Coke. Heroin.

Did Rick's guy deal heroin? I doubted it, but coke, surely.

But won't that raise a huge red flag? You get the guy's number and then he turns up dead? Who do you think is suspect number one?

It wouldn't matter. As long as I wasn't on camera, they'd told me, I'd be fine. They'd clean everything up, and I knew from the videos that it was true. It would just be a coincidence. Why would

I want to kill him anyway? I could tell Rick I never saw him, and hell, the guy would be in the *drug trade.* He'd have a list of people more likely to kill him than a total stranger.

I stood up.

"I'm going to get my phone, ok?" I said to Klaus, who held up a hand in a *stop* gesture. He stood, towering over me, and pointed out of the room. I took his point.

"It's on charge on the bedside table," I said. "I need to send a text. Ok, *you* send the text. Is that what you mean? Look, you can obviously understand me, so just fucking *talk.*"

Klaus' hand turned over and became a *come hither* gesture. I sighed angrily. "This is my fucking house, you know," I snapped. "I don't have to do anything you say." Klaus actually nodded clearly here and held both hands up. *I know,* the gesture said, *it's all up to you. I can leave anytime.* As surprised as I was—this was the most human thing I'd seen him do—I was annoyed by the fact that I didn't have a response. I felt like a frustrated child as I walked ahead of him, leaving the room and climbing the stairs as the larger man followed.

I unlocked the phone, handed it to Klaus, and then dictated the message to him as I got dressed, transferring the small battery packs to my jeans pocket and choosing a t-shirt that hung low enough to cover the cables connecting to the packs. I guess mob informers wore them inside their underwear, but I didn't want to do that and Klaus, fortunately, had gone nowhere near my junk. I guess there had been no need.

I hurried back to the living room to look for fairly recent assault stories while I waited for a response on the drug dealer front. People who'd been caught for being violent types weren't going to change their names or move towns—a lot of them would be proud of it—and wouldn't have been in jail for that long. I could then look them up. They'd probably still have a Facebook profile, and then it'd just be a question of finding an up-to-date address. It was definitely worth looking.

The drug dealer angle might not work after all; maybe Rick wouldn't want to give out the number. He was a close enough friend to trust me—well, only just close enough—but this was someone else's information we were talking about. We'd been drinking buddies for about a year, making the most of his small staff discount at Barrington's, but who knew how his dealer friend would feel about Rick passing out his phone number? Did dealers even give out their numbers to strangers? I suddenly felt stupid. They probably didn't.

Then I heard my phone ping, and Klaus, seated by me once more, turned the phone screen outwards so that I could see it. The conversation was laid out before me:

Rick, do you know anyone who could sort me out something for the weekend? I don't know what I want, and I need options.

The reply:

ha ha yeah I know a guy he doesn't give his number out anymore to new people but you can go see him if I tell him you're coming its fine if I say you're all good here's the address

I told Klaus to reply with:

Can you see if he's in right now?

I went back to my online searches, feeling cold. After a few minutes, the response came back:

yeah hes in for the next hour he says if im vouching for you its all cool to go round hes a good guy

"Tell him... tell him I'm on my way."

This is happening, I thought. *This is actually happening.*

I had my target. A drug dealer. I was going to kill a drug dealer. A drug dealer.

That counts. That's bad enough. It outweighs. It was about the balance, after all.

But how—I wondered this even as I ran to the bathroom to throw up—was I actually going to *do* it?

***

I had the options laid out on the table in front of me. It was now 11:35 am.

A paring knife.

A hammer.

My mother's cheese wire with the little wooden handles on either end.

One to stab, one to bludgeon, one to garrote. I'd been staring at them for ten minutes, and although I'd like to think I *wasn't* stalling—I think I'd be lying if I said I wasn't and who could blame me—it was an impossible choice. Although I really think I'd already dismissed the cheese wire. It sounded like a clever idea, but there was so much that could go wrong with that. At least the knife or the hammer could be a one-hit deal, if done right.

So hammer or knife? Knife or hammer? It was like a Tommy Cooper routine from hell. I'd obviously take both, but one would be a backup, left in my belt perhaps, and the other would be used to do the deed. I felt that trying to use two at the same time would make it harder to focus.

A knife has to penetrate the skin to do damage. It needs to puncture a major organ like the heart to kill quickly, or he'll probably be conscious for a little while afterwards and might fight back. If I catch him unawares with the hammer, right on the back of the head, then he's out for the count at least. Most likely concussed and/or brain damaged and possibly even dead.

It made sense.

Plus, if he's not dead and just unconscious, then you can use the knife.

Could I stab an unconscious man?

You'll find out.

The hammer was small, the kind you'd use to bang nails into a piece of self-assembly furniture. I thought it had enough weight to do damage, yet was still light enough to be wielded quickly.

The reason I'd chosen the paring knife as an option in the first place was because its blade was so short - long enough to puncture as deeply as I thought necessary, short enough to be able to move fast if required - but also because it could slip into my back pocket and not protrude too much. I would be wearing my coat anyway. The hammer would be tucked into my waistband and hang down the leg of my jeans, the head of it obscured by the coat. I had my Dad's leather gloves out, too. I'd washed them to be on the safe side, unsure if they would have any skin particles of his or whatever on the outside or whether washing would make a single fuck of a difference, but I'd done it anyway. I believed the Man in White about the evidence factor, at least as far as that pertained to me, but I didn't want to risk getting my Dad's DNA all over the crime scene. It *was* November, and cold, so it wouldn't look strange to Rick's mate (*not his mate, his DEALER*) if I turned up wearing gloves.

Go on then. If you've chosen, go. Nothing else to wait for. Tool up.

I looked up at Klaus, who was standing next to me and looking as if he were watching my hands. It was hard to tell what his eyes were actually observing, hidden as they were behind his shades. I wondered if he had blue eyes to match his blonde hair. I never found out. I'd be amazed if he didn't, though.

"Look. I don't know if you're allowed to give advice or whatever, but it would make no sense if you weren't," I said to him, speaking as calmly as I could. "As long as you're not actively helping me physically *do* the deed, because that has to be me, right? But you can surely give your opinion?" Klaus, of course, didn't even move a millimeter in response. It wasn't a *no* though or even a headshake. I decided to try anyway. I felt that getting the opinion of someone like Klaus could be a major help. "I think I'm going to go with... uh, with the hammer. I think that's going to be more, you know..." I wanted to say *devastating,* but I couldn't. "It'll do a lot of damage and at least knock him out in one hit. I think there's less potential for *trouble* with the hammer than there is with the knife. So. Do you agree?"

There was silence for several seconds while the black mirrors that were Klaus' eyes bored into mine. I was about to mutter *whatever* under my breath and start trying to calm my shaking hands down enough to undo my belt for the hammer, but then to my surprise, Klaus moved. He did not, of course, take his eyes off me for a single second—Klaus would never do that, not unless he was within grabbing distance—but instead began to walk backwards across the kitchen. It would have looked funny if not for the unusual amount of certainty with which he did this. He walked backwards with the same level of awareness and surefootedness that anyone else would walk forwards. The effect was unsettling. He reached the opposite kitchen counter, where I'd left my father's toolbox earlier after getting the hammer, and reached out with his right hand. He grabbed the toolbox and lifted it as if it weighed nothing—which it certainly did not—and brought it back to the kitchen table where I was sitting, placing it right in front of me.

Now he took his eyes off me—only now I was close enough to be observed peripherally or caught if need be—and began to root around inside the toolbox. After a moment, he pulled out a larger, heavier hammer, and held it before my eyes. I looked from the hammer to his face, Klaus' shades pointing at me once more. He brought up his other gloved hand, holding it slightly below the hammer's head, and then brought the hammer down into his free palm with a weighty *smack.* His empty hand then gripped around the hammer's head tightly, squeezing it and shaking it slightly for a moment.

I got it. I nodded. Klaus did the same.

He then released the hammer's head and turned it around so that the handle was held out to me. I took it while feeling, to my disgust, slightly proud. In principle, at least, I'd chosen correctly. Teacher had approved.

***

Half an hour later, my old Fiesta was pulling up outside a nondescript house in Chapelfields, Coventry. It was a semi-detached building on a relatively nice suburban street. I don't know what I'd expected to find. A crack barbecue going on outside? Guerilla soldiers training child assassins on the front lawn?

Just think of the girls. Just think of the girls. It might even be easy.

That had been my mantra all the way there. My shaking hands were getting worse, and the even-more-present-looming of Klaus, when crammed into the passenger seat beside me, was actually giving me a headache. Well, that combined with the stress, although I really, really *hate* to use that word here. *Stress...* that's what executives get when they're worried about meeting their department sales targets, or what single mothers feel when trying to finish all the shopping in time for Christmas.

I looked at Klaus, already wearing his headphones and looking at a small but bulky hand-held device that was already displaying the view from my badge camera. It was grainy but surprisingly smooth, providing a chest's-eye-view of the steering wheel, the dashboard, and the street ahead through the Fiesta's mud-spattered windscreen. I realized that Klaus was now staring at me, and once he saw that he had my attention, he tapped the headphones once. The message was clear. *I'm watching and listening. Don't get any ideas.*

"Yes, yes, bloody hell, you guys made that clear enough, how many more fucking times?" I hissed, nerves and adrenalin giving my mouth a metallic taste as I spoke.

Think of the girls. You're doing this to save them. Take yourself out of this. You're a remote-controlled drone in this. You don't have a choice. You are not to blame.

The door handle felt impossibly heavy as I fumbled it open and got out, feeling the pain of the hammer's head against my hip lessen as I rose from my seat. I could have put it into my waistband upon arrival, but I didn't want to risk it being seen, or worse, risk chickening out. I looked up and down the street. It wasn't busy, and no one was going to remember an ordinary-looking twenty-one-year-old parking his car and going into a house.

Now just turn around and walk towards the house. Don't think about it. Just do it.

The house had no gate and no low-level wall around its small front garden, unlike a lot of its neighbors', and so I began to stagger my way to the front door on hollow legs. I was about to murder someone. I was about to—

Think about the girls. You aren't here. You are being operated by them. This isn't you. Think of the girls.

I knocked.

The door opened, and a man perhaps ten or fifteen years older than me answered the door, half-asleep. He was wearing a hoodie and what looked like pyjama bottoms, and he gave me a tired smile. His slightly greasy hair was pushed up at the back like he'd only just woken up, and his stubbled face peered at me amiably through sleepy eyes.

"Hello?"

"Hi," I heard someone say, as if from very far away. "I'm Rick's mate. He said I could come and see you?" This strange person's voice sounded normal, not at all as if he was about to throw up on the slippers of the guy answering the door.

"Thought so," the man said, stepping backwards and pulling the door open with him, only briefly glancing over my shoulder to look for anyone watching. The Fiesta, deliberately, was parked ten feet or so along the road, hidden by the neighbors' bushes. "Neil," he said, gently slapping at his chest by way of introduction as I slid into his house. The first wall of security was breached, a killer gaining entry with a weapon, access granted with a simple sentence.

There's a theory in psychology – I've read a *lot* of psychology books in the last decade – that I found absolutely fascinating. It's called *"The Magic Because"*. It's been some time since I read it, but as I recall, an experiment was conducted with a group of people lining up to use the office photocopier, sending in a stranger to ask if he could jump ahead in the line. Something like ninety percent of them said no. When it was tried again on a later occasion, this time giving the pusher-in an obscure reason to do so (*my boss just dropped this on me, and I have like five minutes to get it done, so can I cut in?*), very few people refused.

That's all we need; something to hang our hats on as a reason for what we do. Reasons. I've done a lot of thinking about *reasons.* Neil's reason for letting me inside his house, a complete stranger, just as he would a plumber, carpenter, or pest control officer, was because he'd been told to expect me, even though he had *no idea who I was.* I had a hammer and a knife in my pockets. I'd come to his house solely to murder him in his own home.

"I'm Klaus," I said in response. I'd already decided to use a fake name. I don't know why, given what I planned to do to Neil, but using an alias just felt safer. As I said it, I felt something *shift* inside me, gentle and subtle, but vital. That little change I'd been trying to make. It didn't take it all away, not at *all,* but that small change was there.

This isn't *you. This* isn't *you.* It's *them.*

Neil closed the door behind me. The house was dark. He led me into the kitchen.

***

Chapter Three: A Tough Deal to Close, An Unpleasant Past Reference, and Utilising Existing Market Knowledge

***

I've talked about regrets. *I've had a few*, as the song says. I can see Neil's face very clearly when I think about that day: his slight double chin with its dusting of morning stubble; his skinny limbs attached to a torso that stooped at the shoulders and emphasized his small beer and/or McDonald's belly; a skinny man carrying a slight amount of weight in all the wrong places. The house smelt of almonds. Neil had a faint whiff of B.O. I was a kid, yet Neil had been a man who still thought he was a kid, too.

If none of this had happened—his drug-dealing career aside—the irony is that I think I would have grown up to *be* him.

But it didn't work out that way, and here I am.

***

"D'you, uh, d'you want a cup of tea?" Neil asked, tipping the hoodie's hood back with one hand and scratching at his scalp as he did so. It wasn't a question I'd expected at all. Where was the meth lab in the front room? Where were the Columbians sitting around smoking and listening to Latino music on a tinny radio?

Where was, at the very least, the strung-out girl lying on a pile of rags and filth in the corner, as well as the scummy, wordless associate who sat in his boxers watching an old TV?

There was none of that. It had been hard to see the front room from the outside due to the drawn curtains (strange in any other house given the time of day, but not perhaps so strange in this one). However, as I was led through the front door to the kitchen entrance (bumping a shin against the padded but solid weight of the sofa on the way), I was amazed by the sheer ordinariness of the house. It was a bit dirty and very messy, but this could have been one of my student friends' places. I tried to think of one of their names, but I couldn't. I heard the faint noise of a TV coming from the kitchen. It seemed Neil had been hanging out in there before I arrived.

Said kitchen turned out to be surprisingly clean despite the chips and holes in the ancient (well, '70s era, but that was another era to me) kitchen suite. The linoleum on the floor was heavily bubbled though, and the fridge was adorned with cracked and torn stickers from what looked like '80s cereal box ad campaigns. Through the window to the outside, I saw an overgrown back garden, with a strangely brand-new-looking barbecuing contraption standing at one end.

"No... actually, yes," I said, not wanting any tea at all and then realizing—disgustingly—that I could maybe get him when he turned his back to make the tea.

Don't fucking fool yourself, I thought. *You can't do it yet. You know you can't.*

I have to. It's just after 12 pm.

But—

"Cool. Sugar?"

The question saved me, gave me something I could handle. What was I doing here?

"Uh, two."

Neil was looking at me strangely, pausing with one hand on the open cupboard door. All I could hear was my heart in my ears and my chest. I wasn't surprised by his next question. I thought he could pretty much see the word MURDER written across my forehead, and as I looked back at him I realized that—despite everything—the logical part of my brain was in control, assessing already.

"You all right?"

"Yeah, yeah. I'm just, I'm..." I floundered, looking for the answer. Luckily, honesty was easy. "I just feel fucked, to be honest. I just, y'know, need to relax."

Neil continued to stare for a second longer than I could take. I actually twitched with the tension, my shoulders spasming. Fortunately, he blinked as I did so, and I turned it into a cough. As he fully turned to the cupboard, opening it to grab some mugs, my subconscious brain finished its report and sent it down to the conscious part. It was terrible:

Ok. You have time because you could probably take him even if you didn't *go the surprise route. He's shorter than you, and apart from the gut, he's skinnier than you. You aren't big, but you're bigger than him. You aren't strong, but you're stronger than him. Fuck the hammer. Go close when he shows you the stuff, then put the knife in his neck or stomach. Or if he* does *turn his back, use the hammer anyway and—*

The room actually started to go grey again, and I bit my tongue hard enough to draw blood. It worked and the world came back.

"I know the feeling," he said, fishing around in the cupboard. "Sorry, I'm a bit wary at the moment. I don't really sort out people anymore that I don't know. That obviously means I'm not earning as I was, but geez... I've had a bit of bother with one of Rick's mates before. Guy freaked out on some ket. I don't deal ket to new clients anymore, so if it's that you're after, you're wasting your time. But I owe Rick a favour, so I can sort you something else. He didn't say what you wanted?"

I hadn't expected him to be this verbose. I knew what I was going to tell him in response, an answer ready for *that* question— I'd already planned it—but he'd just brought something up that had caught my attention. I had to take a moment to put my rehearsed answer aside and ask the question. Was he talking about who I thought he was? *Rick's mates* and *ket* in the same sentence... it could only be the same guy. The one that everyone in

Coventry had heard about. We didn't get a lot of that kind of thing in the city, so of course everyone had heard. Curiosity got the better part of me, as always, even through the tightness in my chest.

"Was that... the guy they found stabbed? With ket in his system?"

I'd heard about it on the news, and when Rick had told me that he'd known the stabbed guy—had *worked* with him—I hadn't forgotten it. Clearly, neither had Neil because he froze and stared at me.

"Jesus, would I tell you if it was?" he asked, looking nervous.

"No, no. Sorry. Stupid question. I don't normally do this kind of thing."

"Well, let's just fuck it, let's just get it done then, yeah?" he asked, shrugging and closing the cupboard door, mugs forgotten. "What did you actually want?" He turned to face me, putting his hands in his hoodie pockets. I noticed that.

He couldn't get them out in time—

Time was what I needed. I wasn't ready. I had to get him out of the room for a moment at least. I needed to breathe and push back the kitchen walls that were closing in.

Test him. The confirmation, remember?

"Coke, just need a bit of coke."

A coke dealer. The sort of people they kill all the time on TV.

"'Fraid not," said Neil, shaking his head, looking almost embarrassed for a moment. "Long story. Normally yes, but not for a few weeks now. Rick should have told you that. Speed and weed; ket if I know you. So, y'know, it's only the first two. Which do you want, man?"

I didn't know what to say. I felt cold all of a sudden, thrown.

He's still a drug dealer! He's a drug dealer!

He was. But...

Get him out of the room. Get him out of the room.

"Weed. Uh, please."

I was going to hit this man with a hammer? I couldn't even get my hands to stop shaking.

"Ok. How much?"

What?

"...what?"

"How much do you want? Look..." he paused for a moment, realizing the naivety of the person he was dealing with and probably cursing Rick's name. "I sell it in eighths, right? All the way up to an ounce," he continued, with a slight sigh.

"An ounce," I heard myself say, thinking simultaneously that the larger amount would take longer to get together and also that I didn't have that much money.

Then that's the time to—

"Oh," said Neil, brightening slightly and straightening up. "You know that's gonna be expensive, right? Like..." he paused, and then I *knew*, even in my state of near-catatonia, that he was trying to figure out how much he could get away with telling a clear drug deal virgin like myself. "... £300?" he concluded. The questioning tone of it confirmed it. He was pushing his luck as well as drugs, it seemed.

A drug dealer and *a thief.*

"Yeah, well, that's about all I have to spend anyway so I can't go any higher," I said, the words tumbling out as I marveled at how perfect that sentence was. Acting as if I thought he would try and push things any further, even though I knew he wouldn't. As it was, I was actually relieved. I'd withdrawn my daily maximum from the cashpoint on the way there—£350—and had cluelessly hoped it would be enough.

"Yeah, yeah, ok, that's cool," said Neil, suddenly more eager, his now-nodding head and rubbing - actually *rubbing* - hands giving away his rip-off even more. "Let me see it man. Sorry to ask, but that's the drill." I fished the rolled-up wad of cash out of my back pocket and waved it at chest height. Neil grinned.

"Ok," he said, "pass it here then." I hesitated. Was this how it was supposed to happen? Then my stomach rolled over as I realized that I wasn't actually there for any fucking drugs and that this didn't matter. I unrolled the wad, took out fifty, and handed the rest to Neil. He thumbed through it quickly without a word and seemed satisfied.

"Ok," he said again, "wait here then, ok? Gimme two minutes, ok?" If he said *ok* one more time, I think I would have snapped and done him right then and there. Looking back, I wish to God that he had. It would have made everything so much easier.

"Yeah, that's fine man. Take your time," I said, meaning it. Neil actually smiled in response and practically scurried out of the room, heading back through the lounge. I heard a door open and footsteps going upwards. The drugs were upstairs then, it seemed.

My throat began to tighten. I actually felt it begin to constrict as if someone was strangling me.

Breathe. Breathe. They're going to die if you don't kill this scumbag.

Scumbag. It didn't fit.

He deals drugs and he's stealing your money. Who deserves to live more, philanthropists who do stuff for society or this parasite? And he even said that he normally did *deal coke! Him not having any is only a temporary thing! A coke dealer! A coke dealer!*

The tightness of the hammer's solid head in my waistband was starting to make my hip scream in protest, and I realized that if I was going to use it, I had to get it out *now* while Neil was out of the room. My fingers were weak and shaking so much that I nearly dropped the soon-to murder weapon as I pulled it free. The relief in my hip went unnoticed at my sudden terror that—inexplicably—Neil would appear, magically teleported to the kitchen doorway without any warning footsteps coming from the stairs. If he caught me halfway through pulling a hammer out, stuck at the moment without time to complete the movement, and being unarmed as he responded—

What would he do? He'd probably be more scared than you! And you have the knife!

But that was the problem I always had in any confrontational situation with a stranger. The unknown factor, that which always made me second guess the situation and made my heart race, rendering me useless.

Like the bowling alley guy, the voice in my head reminded me.

It had only been a year or two earlier. Near to Christmas. My old schoolmate Carl and I had decided to go bowling, something we hadn't done for years. In hindsight, I think I suggested bowling as something that we could do because it would make up for any awkward pauses in conversation. We weren't as close as we had been. Either way, we wanted to have a few drinks, and my Mum was going to be over in Wyken anyway at her friend Sheryl's house, so she'd offered to drop us off and pick us up. Boozing with a free ride there and back? Rare, and golden. We took her up on it.

We only had a few drinks during the four or five games we played. As it turned out, it had become competitive, and we were both trying very hard to win. It had ended up being a good evening. A *nice time.* Hurting no one. Mum had turned up a bit earlier than she'd thought—Sheryl had been called to her elderly mother's house, a small slip in the kitchen had occurred apparently—but she'd been happy to watch the end of the last game.

We were in a good mood as we approached the counter to get our shoes back, laughing and recounting funny things that had been said and done throughout the evening, all told to my politely smiling but ultimately uninterested Mother (does anyone enjoy those stories). We waited for the guy who was currently being served to complete his shoe retrieval and carried on talking. We didn't notice the ratty-looking guy who had walked up to stand at the opposite end of the counter. He was dressed in baggy black cargo pants with a matching cap and jacket.

He'd been with a few other guys over in the arcade throughout the evening. Again, we hadn't paid much attention. Why would we? What did we care what a few chavvy rat boys were doing? They weren't our problem as long as they weren't messing with us. The current customer finished being served, Carl stepped up to the counter, and the Rat Boy darted forward slightly and started talking to the slightly surprised looking attendant.

"Mate, I need…" Rat Boy began.

"Sorry, mate," Carl said to Rat Boy, immediately but politely speaking up. "We were next." Rat Boy stared at Carl for a moment, his face utterly expressionless. That was what was so unnerving about it. There was no surprise, no alarm, not even any real sense of *anger,* and yet the response was what it was. The delivery was as flat, quiet, and calm as it was unnecessary, unexpected, and outrageous:

"What you gonna fuckin' do about it?"

He'd spoken like he was asking Carl for the time. My attention was utterly and instantly focused on Carl and Rat Boy now, some kind of ancient and internal survival mechanism kicking in even though no punches were being thrown and not a move had been made. *What? He'd say* that *over* that?

I could sense my Mum—my *Mum,* the guy had spoken like that while my *Mother* was there—standing to my left, completely shocked, but I wasn't looking at her. I was seeing the difference between the two of them. Carl was nearly a foot taller, not a big guy by any means and certainly not a fighter. Carl had never needed to throw a punch in his life. He wasn't a nerd either. He was just an *ordinary guy,* and I could almost read his mind as the wheels of rapid cognition and situational assessment spun like lightning and came to the same confused conclusion as me:

This guy has gone from 0-60 just like that, without blinking and without any rage. This is a pleasant family environment, and yet this person is prepared to bring that darkness here at the drop of a hat. Carl is bigger than him, but the sheer effortless confidence with which this stranger is prepared to fight means that one question is desperately important: what has he got?

"Do? I'm not gonna *do* anything. I came here for a game of bowling, and I'm getting my shoes," Carl scoffed, making a good show of the very idea of a confrontation being laughable and beneath him, but I knew better. I could tell by the change in the color of Carl's skin and the slight shake in his speech. Adrenaline was giving him away. Maybe I could only tell because I knew him, maybe Rat Boy knew too, I don't know. Either way, Carl turned to the guy behind the counter—who was standing there dumbly watching the pair of them, as shocked as we were—as if the matter was done.

My mind was racing. *What has he got, either in weaponry or skills or backup, that lets him talk like that and do it so effortlessly?*

Rat Boy just stood there watching.

This is another day at the office for him, and we're freezing up like virgins. He's better at this than we are, is used *to it, and this feeling is so alien to us that we're stunned. It* is *worth it to him because confronting us is natural and easy.*

We handed our bowling shoes to the counter guy, and he handed us our own footwear back. Rat Boy continued to stand there, watching, not *staring*, but watching.

Afterwards:

"He was just fronting up. That's pretty unnerving though, but if he'd done anything, I'd have hit him," Carl said.

"Can you believe that?" I asked. "Just like that? Ready to fight over that?"

"What kind of a person does that? Says that in front of someone's Mum in a *place* like this? I mean, I beat him up, and his mates come over; it's all happening on camera, then the police are involved... you have to swallow it back and just say *it's not worth it,* but fuck me...."

All well and good, and it ended up being a story with a beginning and no real end, but the story was *in* the beginning. We'd both frozen because there was something *unknown*. It's easy on paper to say, Carl, the bigger guy, swings a punch with his bigger fist into Rat Boy's smaller head, but what if it doesn't end there?

What didn't I know about Neil? Everything. He wasn't a hard case. That much *seemed* to be obvious, but I was planning to try and attack him, and I knew nothing about the man.

No, you're planning to kill *him,* the voice said.

Wouldn't someone like Neil have a little backup ready in case someone came to his house? Wouldn't someone—

Stop making excuses! You're standing in his kitchen holding a hammer! Hide it!

I worked the handle with my shaking hand, walking it up and along the inside of my forearm until the head nestled inside my palm. I could easily conceal it like that, then let go of the head and let the handle slide down my sleeve and into my grip.

I heard footsteps coming back down the stairs, and I screwed up my eyes.

Think of the girls. Think of the girls.

Neil came back into the room, grinning.

"Ok man," he said, holding out the bag of weed. I froze, motor functions torn between lifelong instinct (telling me to take the bag with my right hand) and consciousness stopping that motion in its tracks (knowing that my right hand held the murder weapon). I reached out with my left instead and took the bag from him and suddenly it hit me. I knew how to distract Neil.

"Do me a favour though, bud," I heard myself say, suddenly wondering what Klaus was making of all this, watching and listening from the car. Was he enjoying it? Was he bored? "Did you count that cash? I mean, properly? I just want to check it's all there." Neil did the *it's ok* head shake, waving me away with his hand slightly.

"Yeah, I had a quick count," he said, amiably. "Look, I don't normally even let someone I haven't met come to the house like this, but if Rick's vouching for you then its ok. If it's short, he's sorting me out. I'm in a bit of a hurry, but I can count it again if you want, though."

"Yeah, would you mind?" I, amazed at how normal I managed to sound. "I'm certain it's all there, but I don't want to piss Rick off after he hooked me up."

"Yeah, ok, no problem. I have no issue with double checking what I'm being paid," Neil said with a light chuckle. For a moment it sounded like something my Dad would say.

Does he deserve to die?

He's dealing drugs. He deserves to die more than they do. *That's the whole reason you picked him. You know that this one person deserves to die more than five do. It's him. Do it.*

Neil turned his back on me, as I'd hoped, and began to lay out the twenties on the kitchen counter.

I released the hammer's handle and it slid down my sleeve.

It slid much faster than I had anticipated and shot past my hand, bounced off my foot, and hit the bubbled linoleum floor with a loud and very audible thud.

Time stood still. I remember that very clearly. You may not believe me, but it did. The cliché is sometimes true. I had never experienced a moment like it before or since, even with everything that happened later. I saw Neil's head from behind, frozen in the action of jerking upright and turning to see what the sudden sound was. I felt the dull but deeply intense pain freeze in the process of exploding in the instep of my foot, screaming where the hammer had fallen onto it.

There were no thoughts, at least on a conscious level, but in hindsight I think there must have been thoughts going on *somewhere*, because once time switched back on I reacted in that way that people describe as *acting without thinking.* The subconscious is a strange, fucked up thing.

I spun on one foot to put my back to Neil as he turned away from the money. I dropped into a squat as fast as I could, eyes watering already with the pain from my foot, and let out an agonized cry that I did my best to mask. I tried to turn it into something that was half a moan of dismay, half an old-man-crouching complaint, but it wasn't very convincing. At first, Neil didn't say anything. Squatting, my long-ish jacket blocked the floor in front of me from Neil's view; this meant it obscured the hammer. I scooped it up, and it blessedly slid back up my just-baggy-enough sleeve without effort. Cold sweat broke out across my back.

"Ah, *shit*," I gasped, foot yelling at me, and paused for a moment as if I was looking at something.

"What was that?" asked Neil from behind me. I couldn't hear anything in his voice that I could read.

"Hmm, that was a lucky escape actually," I said, trying to disguise my shaky voice as a light-hearted chuckle. I thought I might have broken one of my toes and my foot was a throbbing block of intense pain. However, it was the cause of that pain that gave my lie any chance of believability. The sound would have been totally different if the hammer had hit the floor. As it was, the hammer's head had hit my foot, which muffled the sound of the impact greatly. The hammer had then landed on the floor handle first, with the head moving relatively gently from my instep to the floor. What would have been a BANG was instead a *thud.*

"Dropped my bastard phone *again*," I said, still with my back to him, pretending to put something (my imaginary phone) in my coat's inside pocket. "I still haven't gotten a case for it; I'm lucky I didn't crack the screen. That's how the last one went." I turned around, red-faced from pain and fear and absolutely shitting myself. I hoped that Neil took the redness to mean embarrassment. Had he seen the hammer?

When I turned around, Neil was looking at me, hands paused halfway through counting the money. He *couldn't* have seen the hammer, surely? It sounded, to my ears, as if there were another hammer in the room, except this time it was my heart smashing away at the inside of my chest.

"What kind of phone?" he asked.

"An iPhone," I replied.

"An iPhone five or six?"

What?

"Uh, five."

A pause.

"You can have my old case if you want."

"... sorry?"

Neil stopped what he was doing and put the rest of the money on the counter. He leant over to his right and pulled open a drawer with a rattle that only ever comes from a kitchen's Odds n' Sods drawer. He fished around in it for a moment, and then pulled out a cheap-looking piece of rubber.

"I just upgraded," he said, holding it out to me. "Had a five and sold it last week. Don't even know why I still have the case, but you might as well have it if you need one. It's only gonna go in the bin."

There was an awkward silence as his hand remained suspended in mid-air, offering me—a stranger—a gift, and I felt ready to faint with relief.

"No?" he asked, slightly confused. "It's a five case."

"Oh. Oh, yeah, yeah, thanks very much," I said, utterly confused, and took it from him. The gift was an act of mild kindness. It was an unneeded item, certainly, but it was thoughtful and well-meant, and it suddenly brought into clarity that which I had truly known from the moment I walked in through Neil's front door. I could not kill this man. *Drug dealer* was a label, and a career that, on paper, ruined lives. When confronted with the reality, however, here was a scruffy man selling drugs on a small scale to consenting adults who wanted to get high. This wasn't a guy getting kids hooked on crack. This wasn't a guy killing people who owed him money. *Did* hard drugs ruin lives? Yes, some lives. Was Neil a part of that world? Ultimately, yes. But the simple fact was that the *drug dealer* tag was not—in Neil's case and in my eyes—enough to warrant his death, and I *needed* a reason that left no room for argument.

Plus—even though it was only a five quid iPhone case—it *said* something.

Hey, a weak, questing voice spoke up, *you know that alcoholism and alcohol-related incidents kill way more people in this country every year than drugs ever do, so you'd be better off killing a bartender—*

I shut the voice up and looked up from the case in my hands to meet Neil's eyes.

Worse still, the voice spoke up again, *putting all that bullshit aside... you're right. You couldn't have done it. No matter what the reason, no matter who you're going to save. You already knew this. You're an ordinary kid. You're not a killer.*

But I had to become one. Somehow.

You just need to find someone worse.

"Thanks, Neil," I said, stepping forward to offer a fist bump and wincing as the pain in my foot screamed afresh. I didn't normally fist bump, but I had a feeling that Neil did. I guessed right.

"No worries, mate," Neil said, and checked the rest of the money. "All good here, as I thought."

"Ok dude, thanks. I'll see myself out, man," I said hurriedly, turning and heading for the door, needing to be out. I'd gone from fear to blind panic to relief to confusion to back to square fucking one, and I needed to breathe.

"Oh, ok bud," Neil said, following me but far behind already as I hurried away, crossing the front room. "You all right, you're limping a bit?"

"Uh, I uh, I just really need a shit," I said, not turning around as I reached the door. "See you around."

***

I opened the car's passenger side door and threw the keys to Klaus. He'd taken off his headphones as I approached, and the handheld device was being placed back inside his jacket. Although the throw of my keys was sudden and at very close range, he caught them in his right hand, his head only moving slightly to track their flight.

"You drive," I said, through gritted teeth. "My foot's fucked." Klaus didn't respond for a second, and then he nodded slightly and got out of the car. His huge frame moved past me, and I slid gratefully into his recently-vacated seat. I pulled the door shut and gripped my foot, moaning... and then realized that I was shaking, hard. Worse, it *wasn't* because I'd nearly killed someone, relieved at the close-but-no-cigarness of committing a mortal sin. Yes, I was full of adrenalin, my nerves and senses were firing as a result of almost getting busted with a weapon in the kitchen of the person I had come to murder; and it *was* a weapon, those of you thinking that it was just a tool. When a hammer is in a toolbox, it's a tool in a stranger's eyes. When it's the only tool you have on your person, when you have it hidden, and you're in the kitchen of someone that you're giving money to for illegal goods, that someone would see that tool as a fucking weapon. But it wasn't that *wow, that was a near miss* shaking, nor was it horror at the bleakness of my situation.

It was disgust. I was disgusted with myself.

I'd been put to the test. *Yes*, it was the dirtiest of jobs, but I had to rise to the awful challenge and take my medicine in order to save five lives... and I'd bottled it.

Don't be hard on yourself, you might be thinking. *You've been asked to kill someone, for crying out loud, are you really supposed to go and do it just like that? Plus, it didn't sound to me like Neil particularly deserved to die. Go have a nice lie-down, you need to give your mind a rest.*

All of which is well and good, but that realization—that I couldn't do it alone, that I didn't have the strength of will to force myself to do it—somehow, that was hard to take. Yet another rubber stamp in my passport to being a Confirmed Useless Dropout Fuck.

You thought it yourself. You need someone worse. That's all.

Maybe so. But at that moment, it seemed to me that a *real* man would just pick a target and get on with it. There were people to save. Fucked up thinking? You disagree? Again, you might be right. But I was the one running this particular show.

I realized that Klaus was staring at me.

"What?" I asked, wearily, undoing my shoe and taking my sock off to inspect my foot. Klaus' gloved hand raised to his eye level, and then his thumb and forefinger came together. They began to rub against one another.

"Yeah, thanks for that," I said, dropping my head backwards against the car's headrest and trying to calm my breathing. That reminder hadn't helped though. Three hundred fucking quid! A week and a half's wages for me! All for some dope that I'd probably never get around to smoking! *Fuck!*

"What do you care?" I gasped, suddenly feeling very thirsty. I was starting to get a feeling that, as long as I didn't try to attack Klaus or out his role in public, I didn't have to worry too much about the way I spoke to him. True badasses in life—unlike the more insecure, less-tough wannabes of the world—don't actually care what less- threatening people do or say. They don't need to. They're probably shit at doing their tax returns, though.

Klaus shrugged in response – *it doesn't matter to me, I'm just saying* – and sat back in the driver's seat, awaiting instructions. My foot was bright red, with a small, dark purple spot at the point of impact, but the bones didn't feel cracked. I screwed up my eyes and took a deep breath, feeling pathetically sorry for myself and trying to be aware of just how much worse the girls had it. I still felt worse for myself though. Fucking little arsehole. I remember that kid. I used to be him, even though I can't imagine it now. I hate him.

What now?

I suddenly realized that I had no idea what time it was. I looked at the clock on the Fiesta's dashboard: 12:32 pm. In just under two and half hours, Olivia's arm would be amputated.

Try and think. Try and be cool. Remember, it's better she loses an arm - all her limbs - than someone being killed who doesn't deserve it.

But it had to be someone worse than Neil—someone bad enough to give me the *cojones* that I needed to actually do the deed, to feel justified enough to break that mental ice surrounding my supposed killing arm—and I was out of ideas.

What makes you angry? If you have to want *to do it, what makes you angry enough to come close?*

The question came out of nowhere and the immediate answers that followed were just stupid.

People that park inconsiderately. Pretentious trust fund hipster twats. Aaron at work. Darren at work. Melinda at work. Fucking Harry at work.

Harry. His smug, grinning face with his jokes that weren't actually jokes, comments carefully prepared to have enough barbs to let you know what they were, but wrapped in a sentence mild enough to a: make you the dick if you took offence, and b: mean that you would be the one in trouble with HR if you did. A weasel. One of only two men that I've ever wanted to take a swing at, and one of only four people that I've ever actually hated.

Could you kill him?

No. I hated him, but he didn't deserve to die.

Are you sure?

I realized that it *was* actually an option. It was a shocking thought, discovering that I was going through my mental rolodex of personal beefs and evolving it into a potential hit list.

I'm pretty sure he's off the list.

And then the rolodex clicked around onto the next entry – the only *other* guy that I'd wanted to swing at – and a very heavy penny dropped. The bowling alley story. It might not have had a real ending, but it *did* have a coda.

It wasn't the actual Bowling Alley Guy. You were unnerved by him and you didn't know what to make of him... but it was the other *guy, his friend, that stung you.*

We were leaving the bowling alley. While we put on our own shoes, Rat Boy had moved away, gone back to his mates who had moved to another part of the building. We couldn't see them anyway. We'd been going through our deconstruction of the situation, telling ourselves that we'd done the right thing and whatever else we could think of to make ourselves feel better as we left. My Mum walked with us and listened, tutting in the right places. As we walked through the door, we saw two of Rat Boy's mates standing outside, dressed almost identically to him and smoking. They stared at us as we walked by and our conversation fell silent, proof if proof were needed that all of our words of bravado were just empty. Or were they? I've certainly learned that instinct is a very, very hard habit to break. If *flight* is your ingrained response, is that your fault? Even when you know afterwards that it was the wrong thing to do?

The silence continued, and we thought that we would leave the situation without further incident. Inside, my relief was total. Then one of them said something, deliberately *just* loud enough to be heard, and another instinct took over when the words reached my ears:

"Fuckin' nigger."

I was already turning before he'd finished the N-bomb, something about the poisonous delivery of even that first consonant letting me know exactly – psychically - where this asshole was going. If it had been just me there, I think I would have let it go, you know. *Just not worth it*, and it really wasn't. I'd been called it enough times in the past—kids learn taboo words and use them against each other—but never really as an adult. I think normally I would have just been more stunned than truly angry.

But my mother was there. And while the word was aimed at me, that vermin knew it would burn her as well. It was the *principle.*

Anger made the difference. Instinct firing in a different way. All logic went out of the window, and I wanted to tear this scumbag's eyes from his head. He was about my size. Would it have made a difference if he was bigger or *badder*-looking?

Probably. I can admit that. The subconscious registers all of these things and responds accordingly. We're just animals.

Either way, I didn't get to know if I could have taken him—didn't get to know if I could take a *real* punch or not, or how effectively I could give one—because Carl caught me around the waist. *My token white friend,* as I always called him. He was tall, remember, and stronger than I was. He had to struggle to hold me, but hold me he did.

I screamed at Rat Boy's fellow Rat, telling him to come and say it to my face and whatever other abuse I could think of. I remember how he just stood there, smoking. He didn't respond, he just watched. He wasn't laughing either, I must add. If he had been, I think I would have chewed through Carl's arms to get to the dickhead.

It was my mother softly talking to me that snapped me out of it. It was like a switch. To hear her having to sully herself by getting involved in this bullshit... it was embarrassing. Bad enough having her witness the incident inside. Bad enough she had to hear *that* word. And having to see her son having a screaming fit—even if she probably wanted to do the same—made it worse. She'd kept her dignity, and I let that *nothingness* of a person make me lose mine. I calmed down, and we left, but not without loudly promising to find out where Rat #2 lived. I disgusted myself by actually crying later than night. I was never sure why. Frustration?

You wanted to kill him. If you'd had a weapon, would you have done it before you realized?

Maybe. And maybe I'd been going about this all wrong. Maybe the Man in White's boss, or bosses, had picked the wrong guy; flight was my threat response, not fight. I wondered if maybe that was why I was picked in the first place, their stupid personality test confirming it. The only way I was ever going to override that instinct was with *another* instinct, a *Magic Because* that came way before any kind of useless logic. I'd been thinking along moral lines, but *only* moral lines as a reason to pick someone, carefully and deliberately leaving out anything that I felt would make it something that I *wanted* to do rather than something I was doing under duress. I didn't want it to be anything that could ever make me think *how much of that was your ugly side?* I didn't want it to be an excuse to take out some long pent-up anger against the prejudices I'd dealt with all of my life, crap I'd had to deal with even though my family had money. Money helps, but hatred like that still slips through the cracks. You still got burned, even if you could comfort yourself with a family holiday in the Maldives.

But maybe some of that personal anger actually *needed* to be used. Maybe some of it was required to get the job done.

Not having access to a rapist or pedophile database—and now that low-level drug dealers were also apparently out—all I had left were people who were assholes. Hell, even The Man in

White had said something along those lines. Technically, the person I picked only had to be enough of an asshole to deserve to live *less than a humanitarian.* But the reality was that wouldn't be enough for me to do the deed. Neil proved it. He wasn't exactly Pablo Escobar, but was enough of an asshole compared to the humanitarians that the girls were. Yet I couldn't kill him, and something as bullshit as an unwanted iPhone case proved that.

So if mere assholery wasn't enough, then I would have to be truly *angry,* too. And who did that to me?

Someone with a contempt for human life... and in the absence of any serial killers on tap, you need someone with contempt for at least some *elements of human life. Someone full of genuine hatred.*

I'd justified it. It wasn't perfect. Nobody would be perfect, but this was enough. I couldn't find a ra*pist,* but I could find a ra*cist,* and I knew exactly where to find one.

***

As sick as I felt—and obviously, as terrified as I felt—I still kicked myself. I should have thought of this earlier. I could have started *this* plan hours before and saved Olivia's arm in the process. The image of a bloodied stump where a finger had been—her screaming face filling a sharp Retina Display and screams emanating from tinny tablet speakers flashed across my mind—and I gripped the hammer in my sleeve tightly. I didn't plan on using it for several hours, but in this situation, it made sense to have it handy in case of problems. *Several hours.* That was the problem. With the new plan, it looked like Olivia was definitely going to lose at least one arm, and more likely, two.

Klaus had his headphones and other paraphernalia out again and was still sitting patiently in the driver's seat. I made sure that we'd parked the car in the most obscured part of the small car park, worried that the building it was attached to was the kind of place in which people kept an eye out for any surveillance. The police had to know about it, even though there was never a lot of trouble here. The pub had its clientele and everyone else stayed away.

The Bonnie Minstrel was a National Front pub. It was just a known thing, so much a tiny part of the city's tapestry that most people didn't even think about it. Every city has a place like this - a dirty old throwback of some kind that is either so titillating, debauched, or poisonous that it's pretty much seen as a joke. Every now and then, someone will ask *is that place even still open* and that will be it. The Bonnie Minstrel, however, was neither titillating nor debauched.

Let me be clear before I say this next part: I don't want to give it more gravitas than it deserves. It's still there today, I believe, and no doubt is still the same grotty old shithole that it's always been, frequented by scared, violent, angry idiots. It's nothing to be scared of, and it's nothing to be talked about in hushed tones. It *is* a joke, and I take no small degree of satisfaction in knowing that with every year the number of patrons dwindles that little bit more. Soon, it will be out of business, and with its reputation, even Weatherspoons wouldn't want to take it over. It'll be turned into a Tesco's.

Now. That being *said...* if you were a young black man, you absolutely did not want to ever go there, especially on a Saturday lunchtime. Even when, as was the case that day, Coventry were playing a late kickoff away (that was a funny time for the team; back then, we didn't even have our own *stadium* for a while, let alone a place in the top four of the Premiership and a Champions League win like we have today). I couldn't be picking a busier or worse time to be going into the lion's den.

Some of my friends had gone to that game. I was only just realizing that they hadn't asked if I wanted to go.

Yes, I had a plan—and it certainly didn't involve committing murder inside a busy pub—but I had no idea if things would play out the way I needed them to. I froze as I put my hand on the car's door handle. I couldn't believe I was doing this. A few years before then, when I was 16, I was sneaking into town for the first time. I'd told my Mum I was going to Carl's. I was getting ready, and like a dickhead, I'd put on my going out clothes at *home.* My plan had been to sneak out with my jacket on over my going out shirt, all zipped up. Idiot.

My dad had walked into the bathroom not realizing I was in there, and despite the standard teenage cry for privacy (*Daaaaad!)* he hadn't turned around. He'd just stood there for a moment, seeing the gel in my hair, the shirt, the open bottle of Issey Miyake, and smelling the overpowering fragrance of it filling the air thanks to my more than generous application of the stuff. I froze. It was absolutely obvious what was really happening.

My dad then quietly closed the bathroom door behind him and crossed the tiled floor. His face was inscrutable... but he didn't look angry. He just looked like he was in deep thought. Then he put his hand on his shoulder and his finger in my face.

"Where did you tell your mother you were going?" he asked, calmly.

"Carl's," I said, shitting myself. Despite his calm demeanour, my Dad could be scary, and repeating the lie like that felt like I was writing my own grounding sentence.

"And are you going to Carl's?" he asked.

I couldn't answer. I just looked at the floor.

"Or rather, are you going to Carl's before you go wherever you're going after that?" he continued. I looked up quickly. He wasn't smiling. He just stared at me with his big, serious eyes.

"Well... yeah," I said.

"Did she ask what you were doing the rest of the night?"

"No," I replied. He nodded.

"Then you didn't lie to your mother," he said. "If you had, you wouldn't be going anywhere." He reached into his back pocket, pulled out a twenty pound note, and held it out to me. "You Skype call me on your phone at midnight, and you do it from living room so I can see you're back at his house. I'll know how drunk you are too, because you're a teenage punk and you wouldn't be able to fake sobriety if your life depended on it. If you don't do all that, you're going nowhere at all for a month. Got it?"

I nodded rapidly, wondering if perhaps Dad had just come back from an early night out himself. That was the only explanation I could think of.

"Yeah, yeah Dad... thanks," I wanted to say more, but I didn't dare in case it broke whatever trance someone had put my Dad under. Maybe Carl had done it. He sighed then, and a small, sad, but wry smile crept up on one side of his mouth.

"Your mother worries," he said, "but we can't lock you up all the time, and you're going to find a way to do this kind of thing regardless. At least this way you do it under my rules."

I hugged him then, without realizing that I was going to do it. He chuckled. "Oh no, don't make me the Good Cop," he said, patting me gently on the back. "Your mother's rules are right, and I back her all the way. This is just one thing she wouldn't understand. She was never a teenaged boy. Or if she was, she's kept that very secret." I laughed then, but when my Dad gently took my shoulders and stepped back slightly, his face was serious once more.

"But listen," he said. "One more rule. For your own safety. And I want you to promise this, ok? The other stuff is up to you—you choose if you want to be grounded or not—but this is something I want you to promise me."

I nodded, confused.

"Don't go in The Bonnie Minstrel. You've heard of it, right?"

Ohhhh. That was it. I'd heard of it, for sure.

"Yeah. Yeah, I have."

"You know why I don't want you to go in there?"

I pulled a slight face and nodded. My Dad returned it, looking very sad for a moment, sorry for his son who *had* to know these things.

"Ok," he said. "Say I promise."

"I promise."

"Say you promise that you won't go in there."

"I promise that I won't go in there."

"Say you promise that you won't go in the Bonnie Minstrel."

"*Geez*, yes—"

"Hey, you aren't trying that lying loophole crap with me," my Dad said, smirking now. "I want it *verbatim*."

I laughed and promised, and it was an easy promise to make because I had no intention of ever going into that shithole. One, because it was dangerous, and two, because there were certainly no girls in there, or at least none that I'd want to try and screw.

And yet here I was, years later, not only breaking my promise to my father, but going inside the Bonnie Minstrel with the delirious intention to commit murder. My parents were far away, and worse, it dawned on me that if my father *were* here, he would stop me from doing this. He would somehow protect me from these men, would tell me to quit, and to let the girls die. I *knew* this. He wouldn't want me to commit murder for any reason. He wouldn't want me to have to carry that guilt with me for the rest of my life. My dad had *endorsed* my actions that night in the bathroom because we were the same. However, were he there in that car park, he would have *stopped* me for the same reason. He would have stopped me because he knew what it would do to me.

I knew that I could never truly go home again no matter how all of this played out.

"I wish I could kill *you*," I said to Klaus, wiping the tears from my face. "I wish I could kill you both." I didn't need to look at him to know that his expression hadn't changed. I got out of the car, took a deep breath, and began to limp towards the pub.

***

Part Two: Overcoming Objections

"Under any circumstance, simply do your best, and you will avoid self-judgement, self-abuse and regret." - Don Miguel Ruiz

Chapter Four: A Change Of Premises, Understanding Different Cultures, and Speaking To The Supervisor

***

I never *officially* moved out of my parents' house when all this was over. I just packed a bag and left them a note saying I'd gone to stay with a friend down on the coast for a few weeks. Most of my old stuff is still at their house as far as I know. Those few weeks turned into a year, with various bullshit phone calls home to give fake updates on where I was and what I was doing. Sometimes I was in Spain, working as a PR guy for a bar and schilling cheap cocktails to holidaymakers. Sometimes I was in France, working as a chalet boy and having a great time with new friends that I'd completely made up. They were pleased and said that they missed me, even though my mother never let me forget that I hadn't said goodbye. After the first year, they began to ask if I could at least come home for Christmas. I made my excuses, but after year three, they started the emotional blackmail. *It's ridiculous. You can manage to come and see us at least at* Christmas. *We'll even pay your airfare.*

Eventually, I relented—I wanted to see them, as difficult as I knew it would be—but got around going home by renting a cheap holiday house in Scotland for two weeks and telling them that it was where I lived. I rented the same place each December for the next two consecutive years—I booked it a year in advance every time—and had them come up to visit each Christmas. It was far enough from home to make it difficult to visit on a whim, and if they asked to come up at another time, I made my excuses and said I was booked for something else. Ironically, I did actually end up living in Scotland for a year, but I still rented that place in December. It was my little house of lies.

Plus, there was still a rule in place. I had to bear that in mind at all times. I had to protect them.

I told them I worked as a social media marketer, a skill they could believe I had picked up online and one they knew little enough about as to be unable to pick holes in my story. They couldn't call—no one in my generation used a landline—and my phone was always off unless *I* called *them*. When I did call, it would be via Facetime, once or twice a month, ten minutes each time. Surface talk. Enough to satiate them, and brief enough for me to be able to stand it. I only allowed the Christmas visits to last for a weekend, making my excuses to keep them from staying longer. That was the maximum period I could spend wearing the mask of my old life; the one that *didn't* have a rotting bag of acid-ridden flesh on the inside. That's how it always felt when I had to pretend I was still the person they knew.

When the dark side of the world comes at you, it's a fist wearing brass knuckles. It leaves you desperately trying to feed on—to draw sustenance from—the beauty around you in an attempt to heal yourself, but you're doing so with a shattered jawbone. You wait for it to heal. It does, but it isn't the same.

For better or worse.

***

It was a different kind of fear I felt as I pushed open the door of the Bonnie Minstrel; one from another plane of existence than the kind I'd experienced at Neil's house. *This* anxiety had started in my legs as I hobbled from the car to the pub entrance, a weakening sensation that had worked its way up and into my chest, constricting and electrifying. It even made me forget about the pain in my foot. By the time I put my hand on the door's brass *PUSH* plate, I thought I was actually, genuinely, going to piss my pants. I knew what this place was, and I knew the way the scum inside would feel about me. I'd chosen this pub because I knew violence would follow - and I was not a fighter.

I actually hyperventilated slightly as the door started to open, but I gritted my teeth with a quiet grunt and headed through it. I didn't look back at the car park or my car containing Klaus and his headphones. I didn't want to risk losing my feeble resolve.

The view before me was as I'd expected. The pub hadn't been even half updated since the mid-80s; it was designed in the '60s. A cheap vinyl-tiled floor covered with furniture of which not one piece—tables, stools, or the bar itself—was free of chips, tears, or stains. Even the yellowing white paint on the walls had random holes and marks everywhere. The only thing in the room that told me which decade I was currently in was the large flat screen TV on the distant wall to my left. In front of me, opposite the front door, was the flimsy-looking bar itself. To my right was a pool and darts area, the last remnants of the insulation tape oche line still clinging desperately to the floor. The only active lighting came from the greyness seeping through the grimy, sticker-covered windows and the TV. To my utter lack of surprise, the flag of my country had been hung over the bar. These fuckers had tried to claim it, as they still do to this day.

One of the great ironies of the human condition is how, in extreme situations, the head and heart can be opposed beyond belief. The relief I felt as I saw that not one of the eleven people in the room was looking at me—their gazes instead fixed on Sky Sports—was like a cooling wave. The response from my head— that I needed them to notice me and that this was not what I wanted—was barely acknowledged.

This won't last.

Anxiety uppercut me again, and I practically fell into a seat at the nearest table to my left. It was that or fall down. My hands were shaking like something out of a cartoon. Only two occupants of the room weren't sporting shaved heads, and one of them was the barmaid.

The men there were of varying ages, some only a year or two older than myself, and some the same age as my father. That was an utterly baffling concept to me at the time. Though none of them were facing me, I could see their profiles as they turned to one another to speak. They looked so fucking *rough*. I don't mean that in a snobby way; I meant that they looked like they fought every day. Here I was, a middle-class kid who had never had a fight in his life, surrounded by people who not only looked like they fought for fun and hated me for the colour of my skin, but would see my presence in their midst as the equivalent of deliberately spilling all of their pints simultaneously.

What time is it?

I looked at my watch. It was 12:56 pm. One hour and forty-seven minutes until Olivia's arm would be cut from her body.

Remember the plan. Sit tight and be ready to run.

I was close to the door at least, as I'd planned, but I didn't know how much use that was going to be when somebody was standing in front of my seated body and screaming in my face. Or if they were blocking the path to the door.

Wait, wait. You can't sit tight. They have to notice you.

They'll notice me eventually.

You can still save her arm!

Yeah, well the arm is expendable! Give me a break for five minutes here!

I sat still and tried to breathe slowly, watching the utter cunts on the opposite side of the room with my peripheral vision. I didn't dare get caught watching them, not yet. I wasn't ready. I went through the plan again, trying to get used to the concept while actually sitting in the pub.

The first version of the idea had been to listen to their conversation and identify who, in a room full of racist scum, was the *biggest* racist scum. Then, once he'd been identified, I would leave the pub, drive to the other side of the road, and stake the building out in the car. This was because I would have a room full of witnesses if I somehow committed murder on the premises. The Man in White had been very clear in telling me that he—or they—couldn't help me if I was caught on public film, but I didn't think this ancient shithole had CCTV. A quick scan of the ceiling confirmed it.

All good in theory, but as I'd driven to the pub I'd been going through my logic and looking for the Magic Because... and realizing that it wasn't there, or at least it wasn't *strong* enough.

If you hear someone being a racist, it could be bravado. It could be someone trying to blend in with a group. They might not mean what they're saying.

Then I would listen for anything incriminating in what they said. Who they'd assaulted perhaps, Chinese takeaway places they'd burned down, whatever.

But that could all be bullshit too. Bravado.

So I'd realized that there was only one way to identify who was scum enough, who was enough of a waste of human flesh so as to be a detriment to society, someone who would attack other people because of the colour of their skin. I had to get one of them to identify himself by actually attacking *me*.

Ideally, it wouldn't *fully* go that far, and I would get out of there before I had to take more than a few punches, but even that was terrifying to someone who had never been in a fight in his entire life. By which I mean me.

None of them had turned around yet. None of them had seen me. It was the most tense I'd ever felt in my entire life, even more than I'd felt at Neil's. That combination of desperately wishing not to be seen and knowing that I had to be.

I watched them without openly watching, observing them out of the corner of my eye, and trying to control my breathing. I looked at the barmaid, expecting her to spot me first and say something to one of the others, but she was as engrossed in the game as everyone else. Five minutes passed. Nothing. It was *excruciating*. I felt a mad compulsion to make some noise, to draw some attention to myself somehow, but I was frozen.

Half-time. They'll all want to go to the bar at half-time.

But that was an age away.

And then one of them suddenly stood up, turned around, and began to walk towards the bar. He spotted me immediately, and I just about shat in my already sweat-soaked underwear.

The guy actually did a double take, believe it or not. It was like something out of a comedy. He'd been laughing as he stood, amused by something one of his skinhead friends had said, and he was still gently chuckling as he made his way to the bar. His eyes had passed over me, his expression still smiling, and had continued their progress to make contact with the face of the barmaid... and then they'd snapped back, his expression somewhere between surprise and anger. I would have laughed if I hadn't been so busy shitting myself.

I wanted to look away, to not antagonise, but I couldn't help but stare back. My eyes flitted to the barmaid, who was now looking to see what Sir Thugalot was looking at. The expression on her face squashed any doubts that I might have had about whether or not my plan was going to work. She looked terrified, but not of me. She was terrified of what was going to happen *to me*. I'm not sure if it's ironic or not that her skin turned even more white than before.

She immediately looked at the other men in the room, then back at the guy at the bar, who was now staring at me with laser-focus. She touched his arm and got no response. She touched it again, gripping it fully now. He looked at her, annoyed, then looked straight back at me and pulled his arm away from her. Using the same arm—the one attached to the hand holding his empty pint glass—he pushed the spent vessel back towards her, indicating that she should fill it. All the while his eyes were locked on me, and all I could do was sit there and not bolt for the door.

What seemed like ten minutes passed while she filled his glass. He continued to stare, using that very particular expression that men of a certain mentality master from a very early age. At the time, I had never seen it before. I have seen it many times since, even with leaving the house as little as possible. I should think, if you are reading this, are male and of a certain age, that you have seen it too. It's unique and unmistakable. It is a perfect balance of threat, challenge, and attempted dominance. Its overriding purpose is to communicate a sense of utter comfort with the concept of violence, whether that comfort is real or not. And this cunt was turning it up to eleven.

I wasn't even twenty-two years old yet, and this guy had to be at least forty-five. I feel my heart rate rising as I write this. Some of it is thinking back to being there again and feeling the fear, but most of it is rage. *Now,* that is. All rage was forgotten back then. I was just a scared kid in a pub full of thugs.

The glass was returned to him, full. He took it without looking, put some money on the bar, and turned away without a word to the barmaid or a pause to collect his change. I watched him sit back down at his table. He shared it with six other guys, with five more sitting at the table next to them, and of course I then saw him say something to the guy to his right. His friend immediately turned around, saw me, then turned back sporting a furrowed brow and slightly open mouth. My skin crawled as he actually began to chuckle, bemused, shaking his head slightly. Then surprisingly, he turned back to the game. No one else turned around.

Two minutes passed.

The friend then turned to the guy on *his* right, slapping gently at *his* friend's shoulder. This other guy turned around, and that was when I finally had to look away. It was starting. But it was also barely past lunchtime, so maybe they wouldn't be drunk enough, or maybe—

My eyes caught the barmaid's again, and I saw that she was still staring at me. The scared expression was still on her face, but now she looked conflicted; I wasn't drinking anything. I was just sitting there. I could almost *feel* what she was thinking. Should she use that as an excuse to get me to leave and thus avoid causing a scene? To do that, she'd have to call across the bar and then *everyone* would look. She didn't have a clue what to do.

And that was when I realized I had to be more brazen.

I stood, feeling detached, as if I was watching my own body hobble its way to the bar, *towards* the group of men who came here to drink in unity of their hatred of people with the same colour skin as me. The barmaid, comically, looked even more panicked. Her eyes widened, and again I could read her mind as she thought *kid, what the fuck are you doing, you're gonna get killed?*

I wondered if this was just a weekend job for her, some extra pocket money, and perhaps she only shared a "slight" racism with these men. Maybe some part of her *was* actually scared for my well-being too, and not just for the potential jail sentence that I could bring to one of her patrons. I didn't know then, and I don't know now. Out of the corner of my eye, I could see my proximity causing ripples among the seated men as I approached the bar, a domino effect of stunned curiosity and growing anger as they turned one by one and stared.

Just like a pack of wolves. That was exactly how it felt.

I reached the bar and placed my trembling hands upon it. I was practically holding myself up.

"Paffof stully, pluzz," I stammered, my throat thick and my lips dry. Confusion penetrated her growing panic.

"You what?" she asked, and looked even more scared. I wasn't just a black kid. I was clearly a black kid with a mental disability; one who had wandered, unknowing, into the worst place in the city that he could possibly find himself.

"*Pint*," I corrected myself, speaking a bit more loudly. "Pint of Stella. Please."

"You got any ID?" she asked, her face flushed as she could feel all eyes on her too. I was dimly aware of a distant amazement in my mind that none of the men had said anything yet. Then I realized she had asked me a question.

"ID..." I didn't. I'd deliberately left my wallet at home, not wanting even the slightest chance of leaving something at a crime scene that could identify me. "Uh. No. But I'm twenty-one. I can tell you my birthday."

She looked immediately relieved.

"No ID, I can't serve you. You can't even be in here. It's the law."

Now it was my turn to panic. I could feel twelve pairs of eyes lasering through me. I wanted to run for the hills, but this was the best plan I had and *time was running out.* My mind raced.

Say something racist to her. *Goad them.*

It would have worked but a: I was too scared to even think about that; and b: that would have been cheating. The Magic Because had to have no loopholes, no catches, nothing where I could say *well you pushed them into attacking you because you said something wrong.* There was nothing wrong with going into a bar; it was their choice if they took that as taunting. It was their ignorance, but if I insulted one of their own? That was giving them an excuse.

Refuse to leave.

I could do that. But then I would get thrown out and that would have been the end of it. Was there any way I could stay there longer and wait for someone's bigotry to make them snap?

The toilets.

"Ok, I understand," I said, my own face so red now that I felt like I would faint, "can... I use your toilet, before I go?" She nodded rapidly in response, clearly happy that I was leaving even if I was taking a pre-exit bathroom break.

"Yeah, but be quick."

"So, I can use the toilet?" I repeated, speaking as loudly as I could without making it too obvious. She actually rolled her eyes in nervous frustration.

"*Yes,* I said yes. It's over there, go." I didn't look to see if my words had been overheard. I knew they had. Even if I hadn't been black, I was a stranger, and in bars where ignorance reigns and tribalism is at its worst, strangers are viewed with the utmost scrutiny. But some cocky punk *black* kid? Fuggeddaboudit.

I turned and limped to the door marked GENTLEMEN—a word that was *definitely* ironic—and pushed it open, feeling twelve sets of eyes nearly pushing me over with the force of their hatred. As terrified as I was, the malice that now seemed to thicken the air around me confirmed one thing, at least: I had made the right choice.

The men's room, as I expected, stunk of piss. The whole thing had, like the bar itself, clearly been installed several decades ago. The walls were entirely white- tiled, with a ceramic urinal attached to one wall and a single chipped ceramic sink mounted on the other. Half a mirror hung above it. A condom machine that looked as if it had been set on fire at some point was hung to the right of that. And to the right of *that...* three toilet cubicles. My breathing was very heavy at this point, and I felt like I might collapse, so I darted into one. I closed the door and sat down on the ancient toilet seat.

I only had to wait. I knew one of them would come.

They'd heard me say where I was going, and I knew at least one of them would be watching to make sure the black kid left. Well, then they would see that the black kid didn't come out again. If they thought the way I *thought* they did, that would be not just a source of curiosity, but of offence; another offence on top of the offence of entering the bar in the first place.

I knew I'd made things worse for myself. I was now stuck. Taking a few punches and bolting for the door would have been bad enough, but now there were *two* doors between me and the outside world. I was sure I wasn't going to get killed, as that would be idiotic even for these guys—doing it on their own turf would be crazy—but a severe beating, one that I couldn't easily escape? That was certainly possible, if not probable. My heart was working away at my ribcage and it was wearing knuckledusters. My cock had shriveled back into my body until it was the size of an acorn.

Five minutes passed.

Again: relief and contradicting desperation. *Come on,* I thought. *Identify yourselves so I know who has to die.*

Ten minutes.

Didn't they hear you? Maybe they were listening, but you didn't say it loud enough?

You did. You definitely did.

Then where are they?

Maybe it's not that kind of pub anymore? Maybe you're wrong?

Fifteen minutes.

The door for GENTLEMEN opened.

Heavy footsteps and a voice.

"What did Mick say? Uh-huh. Uh-huh. He's got experience. He done it, you know, security an' that. Uh-huh. It was up north, some school in the middle nowhere... yeah, I dunno, it burned down or something." I heard the door swing closed and the speaker walked into the room. My skin tightened as I realized I'd made a mistake. I wasn't in the cubicle nearest the door. I was sitting in the one furthest into the room. If the speaker was going to do anything to me, and stood between this cubicle and the door, I would have to get past him to get out. The footsteps continued in my direction, as if they were heading toward the urinal. "Some special school," the voice said. "Rothberry I think it was, something like that. What? I dunno, ask him, he don't talk about it much. He can tell you. He probably knows someone, can hook Dave up, tell Dave I said to talk to Mick. Yeah, no worries darlin'. Is Candy there?"

The man's shadow passed under the door to my cubicle, and he stopped just to the right of it. He was no longer between me and the exit.

Or he's just going for a piss.

That was certainly possible.

"Put her on for me will you, love… hello? Hello darlin'. What are you up to? Uh-huh? Yeah? Oh, that sounds nice. Are you being good? Good. That's what I like to hear. I'll be back in a little bit, so you behave yourself. All right? All right. Put Mummy back on."

I felt myself relax.

He's not that kind of guy. He's a family man. Racist enough to be here, but not racist enough for an assault.

… and then un-relax. Relief and desperation.

So where are the ones that hate enough?

"Hi. Ok. Yeah, all good. Ok, speak to you later." I heard the phone being put back into a pocket full of change and then there was silence.

The feet didn't move away. And then another minute passed and the feet were still outside my cubicle.

The man just stood there breathing quietly.

I tried not to breathe at all.

He's a family man. It's ok. He's a family ma—

Three hard knocks came on the cubicle door. Then silence. My blood turned into water. More silence. I didn't dare speak, although I knew I had to. Here it was. There were two empty cubicles. There was only one reason he was knocking on mine.

Maybe he's checking to see if you're all right.

The knocks came again, slightly harder.

"Occupied," I said, without thinking. I had to say something, after all.

"What you doing?" the voice asked. It was forceful, but it didn't sound angry.

"Using the toilet," I said. My voice sounded weak. I hated it.

"You doing drugs?"

I was surprised into silence for a moment. I hadn't expected that at all.

"No," I said. I heard a rustling of clothes and the shadow changed shape for a moment. He'd bent down and straightened up again.

"You've not even got your jeans around your ankles, so you're not shitting," the voice said with a chuckle that was utterly unpleasant. "And your feet are pointing forward, so you're not pissing. So you're sitting on the toilet doing something. What you doing?" I desperately searched for an answer.

You have to go out there. This has to happen.

But the idea was unthinkable.

"I'm not... I don't feel very well," I said. "I had to sit down for a second."

There was a pause, and then two quick and loud raps on the door.

"Open the door, mate."

"Why?" I blurted.

"Just open the fucking door."

Everything in me bellowed in a deafening chorus of *don't open the door,* both in fear and because this scumbag was telling me what to do, but *this situation was the reason that brought me here in the first place.* I became terribly aware that my rage—as well as my thoughts of anger and bravado outside of the actual reality—had abandoned me. It had been utterly nullified by the twin traitors of adrenaline and instinctive flight response. How could anyone possibly feel this and have a *fight* response? How was that possible?

I remained petulant, at least. I didn't want to do anything this guy told me to, but then I realized that if I opened the door and this guy attacked me, then he was the man I was later going to murder. I would have the last word; the ultimate last word.

So why couldn't I move?

I forced myself to my feet, and I saw the shadow take a step away from the door. My limp noodle of a hand found the thin, lightly rusting bolt on the cubicle door and pulled it back. *Why,* I thought frantically, *why didn't I bring the hammer or the knife?* I deliberately hadn't done so. It had seemed like the right choice at the time. If I had taken the hammer, I might've ended up using it in this exact situation - committing murder in a very public place. I simply couldn't risk it. The choice had made sense at the time, but all I could do now was wish for the reassuring weight and discomfort of it against my hip once more. I opened the door and saw the face of the man I suspected I was going to murder.

I didn't recognize him as one of the men I'd watched turning around to gawk at me earlier. He was older than me by some way, maybe in his mid-thirties. He was slightly taller than me, and not *big*, but bigger than I was. Stocky. He wore a padded jacket over his football shirt too, giving him extra bulk and presence. His face was lean and wiry and slightly red, be it from holiday sunburn or blood pressure. The whites of his eyes were large, and he was staring straight at me. He was physically tense, but did not seem nervous.

I stood in front of him, just staring back, frozen. The silence went on, and I realized that this was part of it for him. This was part of the power play. I knew it and still stared back. I silently cursed my injured foot, my unstable base making me more vulnerable and uncertain.

Just say something to me, a threat, then I can leave. Then I'll know who you are. Then I'll know it's not bravado for the others. I'll know what you are.

Those thoughts might sound brave, but they were not. They were desperate.

"Are you taking the piss out of us or what," he said, and there was no question in the sentence, despite the words. This man had already decided that I was indeed taking the piss.

"No..." I said. "I... no. I just came in to... sit down for a moment because I wasn't feeling well. I feel sick—"

"You don't look it," he said, interrupting, his face blank, his jaw clenching. "You look nervous. What you nervous about?"

"I'm not nervous." The lie was utterly transparent.

"Am I making you nervous?"

Go. Get out of here.

But I couldn't. I had to know, even though it took everything I had to keep standing there. The question was carefully and expertly chosen in the manner of bullies since time immemorial. If I said I was nervous, then I had a reason to be, and if I said I wasn't, then I was antagonizing him.

"I just don't feel well."

"Do you know where you are?"

Oh, I certainly did.

"The Bonnie Minstrel," I said, but I knew I wasn't answering his real question. He did too, and he knew *I* knew.

"Don't be a cunt," he said, and the fact that his face didn't change as he spoke the words did something inside my stomach. "You know who this pub is for, don't you?"

I very nearly played dumb, very nearly chanced it. But the truth was too obvious.

"Yes," I said, "I know, and I'm not trying to, you know, piss anybody off. I just thought, thought that, you know, I was going to be sick—"

"It's not for you. You know this place isn't for you. That's the whole point. It's not for people like you. It's not for you." He was shaking his head, but his eyes remained locked on mine. His words came out quickly. "Not for you," he said again. "You know that. So what you doing?"

"I felt sick—"

"That's bullshit. That's bullshit. What are you doing? Tell me what you're doing. You're not leaving this toilet until you tell me what you're doing."

To my utter panic, he took a step forward, planting his feet against mine. His eyes had widened. To my utter shame, I leaned away.

This was a mistake. You didn't think this through at all.

A horrible realization washed over me in that moment. My anger, my big plan to anchor me and steel me and power me through whatever I had to do, had abandoned me. I thrust about in the darkness of my mind for some steel, and there, in the moment, I found none.

"I think you're taking the piss," he said, and he was breathing heavily now. "Student, are you?"

"No, I have a job, I work at the--"

That was when his head cannoned forward and butted me on the bridge of my nose with devastating force.

At this point, some of you may be reading this and thinking *so what? Someone in a pub toilet giving you shit? Why didn't* you *just head-butt* him *in the face first and be done with it? All in a day's work.* If so, you aren't like me then, and I wish I had that part of you in my brain, but I didn't, and I don't. I know that now.

The world went white, and I really did feel sick as I fell backwards, my legs buckling and my arms flailing pointlessly, attempting to stop my fall to the grubby tiled floor of the toilet cubicle. My head glanced off the edge of the toilet bowl and my teeth smashed together, the two-year-old porcelain veneer attached to my right front tooth splitting in half. I hit the floor hard, my head to the right of the base of the toilet as blood jetted out of my nose and my vision became blurry. All I could taste was copper and thought wasn't possible.

The impact of the blow to my face wasn't just shocking physically. I had never been attacked so severely in my life. The idea of the world where I could have a nice conversation with my Dad in the bathroom—the world where I could perhaps have a genteel middle-class family meal—flashed before my eyes like an image of utter madness. How could that world exist when my nose had been smashed by a man in a dirty pub toilet?

I put my hand to my face and it came away as a scarlet glove; I will never forget seeing the blood pooling at the edge of my watch strap.

"Uh," I gasped, blood spraying from my top lip as my spastic breath burst forth, "uh, uh... uh." I rocked on the floor like an upended turtle, blinking.

Stunned, was the first thought that came through, detached and observant. *This is what they mean when they talk about being stunned.*

I lifted my head, only half-seeing, and saw the man standing in the cubicle doorway. He was watching me, but he was still. His face was expressionless again; that was the worst thing. That was when I knew that—perhaps *because* of my stunned state, a piece of clarity in the chaos—that I could murder this man. He pointed a finger at me, and my hands automatically came up to show submission.

"You're taking the piss," he said again. "This is what happens. All right? This is what happens. You're not coming back here, are you?"

"Muh. Muh," I said, unable to get the words out, so I shook my head even though doing so made white spots dance before my eyes.

You have to get out of here.

It was too late now, but I was dimly aware that he'd made his point. He could now go back to his table and tell them how he'd shown me what was what.

You have to get OUT of here. Your face, what has he done to your face—

"'Cos you fucking know, right? You fucking know what happens?"

I nodded, blinking and wide-eyed. Why couldn't I get my eyes to focus?

The man stepped forward into the cubicle. I can remember the sight; the walls of the cubicle trapping me on either side and my assailant looming over me. *Kick him in the balls,* a distant part of my mind said, but even if I'd been able to get my legs to work I wouldn't have done it. If I was being offered a chance to check out of this conflict with only *this* much damage being done, I was desperate to take it. I think about that too sometimes, when the nights don't seem to end. What was the line from The Shawshank Redemption? *Time draws out like a blade.* It really does.

"You know, right?" His eyes were wide again and his breathing was speeding up.

No—

His boot came up and stomped down on my groin. I cried out. This time the pain was of a completely different nature, and I felt my eyes prickle as I thought for a horrible moment that I was going to cry.

Not that. Anything but that. You will give this cunt your submission, but you will not cry for him.

"You fucking *know*, right?" the man said, and he was almost shouting, leaning down, his victory giving him some kind of animalistic anger. *You've won,* I remember thinking, *what the hell are you getting so angry about?* "You don't fuck about!" His foot came up again, but I could see by the way he raised it vertically rather than swinging it back that he was planning to stomp somewhere on my leg - the leg attached to the foot that I'd injured at Neil's. I clumsily tried to move it, but it wasn't enough. His boot came down on my ankle, and I felt something crunch slightly. An almost wet, warm-feeling pain ballooned at the spot where he'd stomped. It was a heavy pain, the type where you *know* something isn't going to heal well.

I tried to sit up, to begin my attempt to get past him somehow. The man pointed at me again. "You don't! Fuck! About—"

Suddenly, the man seemed to dart backwards out of the cubicle. I blinked, wondering if it was my eyes or some kind of concussion-based illusion, but it wasn't anything of the sort. The man had actually travelled several feet away from me, stumbling as he went. I thought he was going to hit the far wall, but he managed to get his feet under himself and stop. His face reddened even more deeply as he quickly straightened up, his chest sticking out. He was looking at someone. Someone who had pulled him off me? Whoever it was, the cubicle walls were obscuring him from view.

The man was still breathing hard, his eyes now looking ready to burst from his face... but less certain, I thought. He wasn't backing down from whomever had come in, but that confidence, that terrible *confidence* wasn't *quite* there anymore. The only sound I could hear was the man's heavy breathing.

"D'you fucking want something?" the man said, and he was *trying* to sound sure of himself. It didn't quite work. There was no response. The man moved slightly towards whomever the newcomer was, unnerved by the silence and only being capable of thinking in terms of attack. "I said *do you fucking want something?*" It was almost a shout.

And then I noticed the man's line of vision and just how much he had to look *up*.

The man moved forward again, lost for anything else to do.

"What the *fuck* are you supposed to be dressed as—" The sentence was cut short as something hit the man in the chest, hard, and he staggered backwards like he'd been shot. There was a strange secondary effect to the blow, as if the man felt the force of it first, and then a moment later, the *damage* it had done. He began to open his mouth again, the finger began to raise in yet another point, and then a hand went to his chest. He made a little strangled noise with his mouth. He then wheezed in a huge gulp of air and straightened up. He swung a pointless, limp-armed punch.

Klaus stepped into view and almost lazily stopped it forearm to forearm, then snapped his blocking arm straight, propelling his fist perfectly into the man's nose. If I thought *my* nose had been damaged, my assailant's nose practically exploded in a burst of red. Klaus then swung his arm over the man's, locking out the elbow of his "opponent"—Klaus had done all of this with one arm—and then made a sort of thrusting movement with his shoulder. There was an audible *crack* and the man began to scream. Klaus let go and stepped back, and the man's arm fell in a way that it wasn't designed to. He screeched and dropped to his knees holding his broken limb, looking up at Klaus with desperate eyes. Klaus' impenetrable sunglasses and expressionless face looked back. Seeing nothing in Klaus' face—to my total amazement—the man then looked at me.

"That's it," he gasped breathlessly, his voice high-pitched with pain. "That's enough, that's it." I stared back at him, more stunned than ever. Klaus moved in around behind the man and wrapped his jacketed arm around his neck, his other hand going behind the man's head. In his huge black coat, Klaus looked like a beast, my assailant his prey. "Thasssit!" The man continued pointlessly, gurgling the words through gritted teeth as he began to run out of breath. "Thassenuff! Thassenuff, thassit!"

"Klaus!" I gasped, finding my voice. "Don't kill him! I need... I need to..."

Klaus looked up at me and furrowed his brow, shaking his head briefly. He almost looked annoyed. *Don't be stupid.* He looked back down at the man, watching him diminish.

"Thassy... thass..." the man mumbled, his struggles lessening, his eyes fluttering. Klaus was putting him out. What the hell was going on? Why had Klaus intervened? Was he allowed to do this? Was he setting the guy up for me or something, making it easy? The man's fading eyes settled on me, and I knew he was, in a way, in the same boat as me. He was wondering what the fuck had just happened. A thought came to me:

You'll never know, asshole.

I then remembered why he *definitely* wouldn't know, and I felt even sicker. Where was my fucking *anger?* The man's eyes fell shut and his cries diminished to nothing. Klaus held him a few more moments and then simply let him go, standing up as the man's body slid limply off Klaus' legs onto the crappy tiled floor of this racist fucking pub.

Klaus looked down at me and held out a gloved hand. Feeling as if I was made of feathers and that my head and balls were being beaten up from the inside, I struggled upright and took it. He pulled, lifting me pretty much straight up with very little effort, but as soon as I put weight on my bad foot I knew something was now a lot worse. The man's stomp on my ankle had added significantly to the damage. Pain lanced up my leg, and I fell sideways against the cubicle wall, crying out slightly. Klaus' brow furrowed again, but I could see that it wasn't from concern. It was annoyance. Normally I would have yelled *fuck off! He just stomped my ankle!* But the wave of gratitude was washing over me as I began to fully realize what Klaus had done. He had absolutely saved my ass. Despite my shame and shock, I was desperate to thank him.

"Klaus... how come you... thank you," I said, wincing at the throb from my ankle. "I can't believe... I didn't think you could, y'know... interfere..." Klaus shook his head slightly and held up a hand. *It's not like that.* I didn't know what he meant, but right then I didn't care. Klaus took out a packet of something that looked like Wet Ones from his seemingly endless number of coat pockets and began to go around the surfaces in the room with them, wiping the walls, tiles and cubicles down with practiced speed and thoroughness. I watched, open-mouthed.

Jesus.

I wanted to look at my face. I hopped gingerly from my cubicle and around the unconscious man on the floor, and as I did so, Klaus moved into my former hiding place and began to wipe over every inch of it. He then came out and scooped up the racist under his armpits, dragging him into another cubicle and propping him up on the toilet seat. He then exited and pushed the door closed. *Getting him out of the way,* I thought. If some of the other guys came looking for their buddy, at least they might think he was taking a shit. Already, the only evidence of a fight was my blood-covered face. I needed to wash it.

Wash your face. Wash off what you let him do to you.

I couldn't think about that right now. I only could think about what needed to be done next, and I knew the more I thought about that, the easier this whole nightmare would be. Plus, I realized how much blood was in my mouth, and I wanted to get rid of it. As I hopped over to the sink—feeling like I could collapse at any moment—I went to spit into it, but heard Klaus move hurriedly from behind me. I stopped and turned to see him leaning around me to run water from the tap. He then nodded at me. *Now you can do it.* He waited until I was done, the water catching and immediately washing away my bloody spit, but then I saw my face in the mirror. I gave a little cry of surprise.

The lower half of my face was a crimson mask. My nose, to my great surprise, wasn't actually bent off to one side; I wasn't even sure it was broken. But it was swollen hugely, the centre looking as if someone had managed to fill it with cotton pads. It ached and pulsed.

Sure. You're not too bad on the inside. *You remember how you tried to beg him to stop?*

Just get on with the job.

I looked at Klaus and pointed to my nose with a shaking hand. My whole *body* was shaking, for that matter. Was this shock? This was nothing like the films. People got pistol-whipped and carried on fighting. A head-butt and a kick in the balls and a stomp on the ankle and I was trembling like a scared dog. *Christ.*

"Can you... you know how to check this, right?" I asked, turning to Klaus and pointing to my nose. "You know medical stuff? Like field medical stuff, right? Like in the army? Surely you must." Klaus, of course, stared back for a moment, then lifted his hand to my face, pushing his gloved finger onto either side of my nose. I flinched, and my nose ached where he pushed, but there was no sharp pain. He then seemed to inspect my face, head slightly on one side. "Not broken?" I asked. Klaus shook his head. "Wait," I said, thinking again. "Does that mean *not,* not broken, or not broken? Wait, ok, *is my nose broken?*" Klaus paused for a moment, and then—sarcastically—he shook his head.

"All right... don't take the piss," I snapped, turning to hold my still shaking hands under the running water. "You know, this would... *uhhh*... all be a lot easier if you dropped the vow of silence act. What's that all about anyway?" I winced as I washed my face. The blood was still trickling from my nose, but less so now, and I thought I could stop it once I cleaned up and got some tissue to hold against my nostrils. My face, I'd been head-butted in the *face*...

Middle-class pussy.

"You can obviously understand English, so why not just..." A thought occurred to me, one that I'd pondered before now returning with so much weight behind it that I stopped what I was doing.

Klaus' whole Russian secret service agent look. The Man in White's Bond villain outfit. Klaus' Odd Job routine too, come to think of it. Really... I mean *really...* wasn't it all a bit... *theatrical?* Didn't it seem so contrived?

Their employer has people killing for no other reason than to see what choices they make. Do you really think he's above making his employees dress and act like something out of an '80s action movie?

This was true. I realized that Klaus was watching me, and I wiped the last of the blood from my face. He handed me a wad of tissue paper that he'd already taken from the cubicle.

"Thanks," I said, pushing it against my nostrils before the blood flow could start again in earnest. Klaus didn't respond, leaning around me again to turn off the tap and then give the bowl a good wiping. I moved out of his way, and looked from the closed cubicle door to Klaus.

The wiping. He's pre-empting things. I told him the plan on the way here, so he knows that I'm going to get this guy later. He's removing any physical evidence that I was here now, *erasing any possible connections for* later. *When the guy turns up murdered tonight, you can bet the cops would be swabbing the room where he was knocked unconscious earlier in the day to find clues. Klaus is pre-empting it. Fuck me. Fuck ME. This is HAPPENING.*

I leaned back against the sink, taking deep breaths, and watched as Klaus finished up. Once he was done, he stood in front of me and nodded.

"I didn't know you were allowed to do that," I said again. Klaus didn't say anything. "*Are* you allowed to do that?" I asked. Again, no response. It was still annoying, but I was still strongly aware of how much of a beating he'd saved me from. As far as I was concerned—in that moment—he could have taken a shit in my hand, and I still would have said *good man Klaus, please can I have another.*

"Ok, whatever, but thank you," I said.

Think about what's next. Everything else will be easier that way.

"Listen," I said, "we need to get out of here before people come in and start asking questions." My voice sounded as if I had a cold and there was a tremor in it. "I think... I might have to lean on you, my ankle... I don't know what he's done to it, but if everyone in there sees me come limping out of the toilet this badly, they're going to know what happened and wonder..." I sniffed on instinct and regretted it, my nose throbbing harder in response, "...wonder where the other guy is that followed me in here. I've cleaned my face up as best I can. How's it look?"

Klaus gave a very little shrug in response. I took that as meaning *whatever, it's ok.* "I'm not worried about them doing anything, not with you here. I'm worried about getting out of here before they find an unconscious man and then get my car's plate," I snapped. "They can take a passing interest in a huge guy looking like a spook supporting a limping black kid in a National Front bar, but if the kid has a clearly busted up face, they're going to go looking for their mate when he doesn't come out of the shitter, ok? *The car has to be gone by the time this blows up.* Now can I get away with hiding my face with my phone, as if I'm talking, like this?" I showed him. Another shrug in response, but this time with a little bottom lip sticking out in thought; *yeah, that could work actually.*

The difference between matters that Klaus responded to with an opinion and matters that he ignored seemed to be almost random. "If I walk on your other side," I continued, "and you walk between me and them where they are down that end, then that should be ok. That should hide the limp a bit, too. Then we get in the car and burn off as quick as we can. *Jesus,* my foot. You'll have to drive again. This time my foot's way worse. I can barely put weight on it." Klaus paused and nodded that he understood.

And what next? I thought. *What about after that?*

Then we wait and—

We had a problem. Sure, the plan had been to wait and follow whoever started something with me once they left the pub. But now we had to get out of here before this guy was eventually found—or before he could cause a stir himself—and people spotted us in our car watching the place.

Imagine if they got the car's plate. Jesus.

But, if we had to get the car away, and we couldn't risk getting caught hanging around outside—in case the cops showed up to investigate an assault on the man we would later murder—how were we going to follow this scumbag home?

The good news was that almost certainly they didn't have CCTV, and even if they did, I felt confident that the Man in White's people could do something about fixing that issue in a cheapo shithole like this. The bad news was being unable to wait for—

His wallet. Get his address.

Of course!

"Klaus, can you get the guy's wallet please?" To my amazement, Klaus shook his head.

"What?" I barked. "You just beat the crap out of this guy, but now you can't get his wallet? I'm not *stealing* from him. I just want his fucking address!" Again, Klaus shook his head. What was going on here? He wasn't allowed to help me? Or just *wouldn't* help me? Then what was all the business about him kicking the shit out of our racist chum? "You have got to be kidding. I can barely stand!" Klaus just stared at me. There was nothing else to say. Scowling, I half limped, half hopped over to the cubicle with the unconscious man in it. I closed the door behind me, in case anyone came in.

Getting the wallet was extremely difficult, but fortunately, Klaus had done enough of a number on the guy that he remained unconscious throughout. Standing on one leg and leaning against the cubicle wall, I tipped the guy's body forward at the waist—he was spark out remember, still sitting on the toilet seat where Klaus had propped him—until his upper torso slumped against my outstretched thigh. Wincing and grimacing with the effort, with my jacket's sleeve around my fingers acting as a makeshift glove to prevent leaving any prints, I managed to get my hand far enough under his backside to fish his wallet out.

I flipped it open. I became very still as two pairs of eyes stared back at me from behind a clear plastic window.

I did some impromptu and unwelcome detective work, putting the photo and the dim memory of earlier, overheard dialogue that had come from the other side of the cubicle door:

"I'll be back in a little bit, so you behave yourself. All right? All right. Put Mummy back on."

And I knew, again, that I couldn't fucking do it. A rule had just been added to my list, one I should have thought of from the very start. I let out a moan of dismay that was almost a sob, and let the piece of walking human shit's wallet drop to the floor. I slumped myself now, my head banging back against the cubicle's partition wall. I felt like screaming.

"You lucky son of a bitch," I said, almost in a whisper. "You fucking lucky scum."

You couldn't have done it anyway, the voice said in my head. *Where was your anger? Wasn't that the entire point?*

I could have done this guy. I would have remembered what he did. I'll show you. I'll fucking show you.

Anger built in me out of nowhere, a sudden fury that was a good five minutes late in arriving. It was powerful, intoxicating, and to this day I wonder if it ever would have arrived if Klaus hadn't been there in the room to back me up. I don't know. All I *do* know is that in a moment of absolutely perfect timing, the racist began to wake up. He was blinking, but unmoving. His eyes hadn't even focused on me yet. He was conscious, yet barely aware of anything.

It had all been too much, and this man, this *vermin,* was awake, and practically helpless. Looking back and writing this— *feeling* those feelings all over again—I'm amazed that I managed to wait until he saw me. I *wanted* him to see me. His brow furrowed and his mouth opened slightly. I then dove forward, my body weight entirely on my knee as it slammed into in his groin, and smashed my elbow down onto his forehead as hard as I could. He didn't make a sound. I don't even know if he stayed conscious after the first hit. I elbowed him again and again all over his face. His eye sockets swelled up like a baseballs made of meat and bone, and a small part of me left as they did. Some tiny but vital piece of my soul stayed in that filthy cubicle in a building that should have burned down a long time ago. I didn't realise until afterwards that I had been crying as I hit him.

I leant against the wall when I was done, holding my throbbing elbow and noticing distantly that the sleeve of my jacket now had blood on it. Fortunately, it didn't stand out against the darkness of the material. I tried to calm down, but the tears kept coming. I tried to stop as much as I could, jamming my other sleeve into my mouth to muffle the sobs, and it worked to an extent. I felt utterly wretched and sorry for myself, even as I knew I should really be feeling sorry for the girl who was about to have her arm cut from her body because I'd failed. Again.

I heard someone else come into the room and so I lifted my good foot onto the racist's leg, pushing up so that whoever had come in wouldn't see two pairs of feet under the cubicle door. I don't know what this person made of Klaus or what Klaus was doing when the guy entered, but whoever it was went for a very quick piss indeed and left without even stopping to wash his hands.

When he'd gone, I managed to get myself under control enough to hobble back out of the cubicle. If Klaus noticed my red eyes, he didn't acknowledge them. I looked at my watch. 1:47 pm. One hour, thirteen minutes to go until the first amputation. I needed a rethink and a big one at that.

You have to be kidding, don't you? You can barely think straight.

"Come on," I said to Klaus, quiet and sniffling. "Like I said. You stand on their side of me. I'll pretend to be on the phone. Let's go. Come *on,* let's go." Klaus came and stood next to me, and I leant my weight on his shoulder. I tried to make my gait as normal as possible before we got to the toilet door, but it hurt *so much.* I wondered what the guy had done to my ankle. I tried not to think about it.

I could feel people watching as we made our way across the pub. I didn't dare look, of course, instead staring straight at the exit making *uh-huh, uh-huh* noises into my phone as if I were listening to someone. As the door opened to the world outside, pushed by Klaus' shovel of a hand, I felt as if I were emerging out of a dungeon. I wasn't relieved—I felt too dirty for that, too smothered by my situation—but I felt like I could breathe. I could hobble more openly now that we were outside, and in that fashion, we made our way to the car.

"Can you at least *drive?*" I asked Klaus, scowling but not looking at him. "You can't get a wallet, but you can *drive* us out of here, right? You're not supposed to let me get caught. If you don't drive us out of here, we're going to get—" Klaus was already leading me around to the passenger side of the car and opening the door. "Right," I said, feeling a little stupid, "good. I can't drive like this, you see..." He moved away and around to the driver's side of the car. I got into the passenger seat awkwardly. Klaus was already seated and belted and staring at me.

"What?" I asked after a moment or two of this, I realized I hadn't thought that far ahead. "Oh. We're going home. To my home. I need to... let's go home. Uh...."

What difference is it going to make? You can't do this. You know you can't do this.

"Home. Let's go home so I can think."

Klaus turned the key without a word, and the car reversed quickly across the car park. I looked in the rear view mirror, watching the door to the pub and expecting racists to pour out waving pitchforks and flaming torches, carrying the beaten and unconscious body of their compatriot aloft in indignant rage... it didn't happen. The match was still going on, after all. I suspected that our mutual friend might be in that cubicle for some time. The bonds of their brotherhood, it seemed, were even weaker than I'd thought. Even so, I still breathed a sigh of... not quite relief. I would not feel true relief again for a very long time. I put my head back on the seat, trying to ignore the pain in my ankle, and my mind went blank as Klaus drove.

But Klaus didn't drive me home.

***

Chapter Five: Protocols And A New Schedule, A Much Needed Cosmetic Overhaul, Key Advice From An Experienced Mentor, and An Exciting Breakthrough

***

I've thought about killing myself a *lot* over the last decade. Don't misunderstand; as I said, I don't feel *real* guilt, in as much as I know I was put in an impossible position. I *know* I could have handled things a lot better—even though saying that sounds like I'm talking about a bad business decision or an argument with a fiancé's family, and not the murder of another human being—and I have a *lot* of regrets. But I don't think I deserve to die for it. That's my point. I'm not a bad person. I'm just someone who tried to do the best he could, but I've known ever since that actually, I could have done a *lot better.* Hindsight is not a wonderful thing. It's a dirty son of a bitch.

But no, I thought about killing myself because, for a long time, I could barely breathe or get out of bed in the morning. And again, I wonder: the same people that can fight at the drop of a hat, who can take a beating and brush off the mental side effects as if they were nothing. Soldiers, or at least the ones that don't get

PTSD. There are *executioners* in the American states where they still have the death penalty *and it's part of their job to administer it.* And they, presumably, all sleep fine at night.

When people hear about others who have committed terrible crimes, their response is often something like:

I'd kill them. Give me a gun and I'd do it myself. I'd pull the lever. I'd flick the switch.

Perhaps you've even said it yourself.

Try looking into the eyes of the people you're killing as you do it. Try watching the light in there dim as they go to a place they can never come back from. Try seeing everything they ever were, everything they are, and everything they never will be disappearing into nothing, nothing, *nothing,* and watch as they realize it's happening and watch while *you know that you are the reason it's happening.*

Watch, even if they deserve it.

Then try to sleep.

***

Klaus pulled the car over, and I came out of my trance. There was no way we could have driven home yet, surely? I looked around us. I was right.

He'd stopped the car on some residential street that I didn't recognize. It was nice, with lots of detached and semi-detached houses, and cars of medium-level expense on private driveways.

You could bust in the door and kill anyone inside those houses. Then all this would all be over.

"What's happening?" I asked, feeling very confused and a little afraid. Klaus apparently knew something I didn't, and I wasn't certain whether or not I was in trouble. I suddenly felt very foolish for operating under the assumption that the rules they'd given me were all there was to worry about. Were they men of their word? Why would I believe the statements of a white-suited lunatic who apparently worked for an even bigger lunatic?

Klaus got out of the driver's seat and walked around the front of the car to my side. I froze. For a moment I thought about running, but I knew that would be pointless. I could barely walk. Klaus then opened the passenger door and squatted down, still outside the car. He extended a gloved finger and pointed at my injured foot. I didn't know what to say for a second.

"Yeah," I said, sounding as uncertain as I felt. "That one. It really hurts." Klaus' fingers flicked inward in a come-hither gesture. Feeling like a child, I extended my foot towards him, my leg now poking out of the car.

Does Klaus have medical training? I wondered. *He didn't seem too thrown at all by what you said about field medicine. Face it. You know absolutely nothing about the guy.*

I winced as he took my foot in his hand, but he did so with such surprising gentleness that I didn't feel any difference in the pain. He felt gingerly around my ankle with his other hand and turned my foot very carefully. It hurt at one point, I let out a gasp, and he stopped. His finger then went straight to a particular spot and pressed lightly. That hurt a lot more, and I let him know about it. Klaus nodded, placed my foot back inside the car, and stood up. He then closed the passenger-side door and made his way back to the driver's side.

"What's the verdict?" I asked, as Klaus settled his bulk back into the driver's seat. Of course, he didn't say a word in response, but surprised me by taking an iPhone out of his jacket pocket. He unlocked it and began tapping away.

"Wait, what are you doing?" I asked, the fear returning, but again there was only silence. After about a minute, Klaus placed the phone in his lap, its screen locked, and then stared straight ahead through the windscreen. Fear got the better of me and, as if making up for its shameful performance from earlier, managed to turn into anger, albeit about half an hour after it would have been fucking useful.

"I asked you a question!" I snapped. "Yes, yes, I get it, the enigmatic silent routine, whatever! It's gotten old! It doesn't make you cool. It just makes you annoying! And rude! What the hell is going on now?" No answer. He just kept looking straight ahead. I wanted to kill the guy. I looked at my watch. 2:15 pm. Olivia's arm was coming off in forty-five minutes. "If you're putting me on the clock, and you've taken me here when I didn't even want to *come* here, then stop the fucking clock! Stop the clock! This is bullshit! Stop the clock!" I was yelling now; my hands balled into impotent fists.

Then the phone on Klaus' lap started to ring. It was a Facetime call—video—and I could see a name onscreen:

JOHN DOE WOULD LIKE FACETIME...

I had a sinking feeling that I knew who John Doe was. Klaus accepted the call and picked up the phone, turning the screen to face me and revealing a smile that I already knew would be there. I will always remember that moment. I felt the small hairs on my neck stand up and my spine went cold. I mean it was as if someone had poured water down the back of my jacket. I'd never experienced that before and never have since.

"Chris, Chris, hi," the Man in White said, his face lit solely by the glow of his own phone's screen. The lights were off in the room behind him, presumably to give away nothing about where he was. It gave the overall effect that he was talking to me from a cave. His sunglasses and grin seemed to bulge onscreen, and for a horrible moment, it felt like I was talking to a troll in its lair. "Didn't think we'd be talking so soon. I hope you're doing ok, you know..." His finger came into view and tapped the side of his forehead, and I noticed that wherever he was, he wasn't wearing his gloves. "I can only imagine what an unsettling experience this must be for you. Just try and remember why you're doing it. That's what I always tell our Participants. Focus on that."

"What's happening?" I asked, my mouth dry. I had, however, taken some strange sense of relief from his words. If he was giving me encouragement on how to better handle the situation, it meant that my own situation was not, for wont of a better phrase, coming to a blunt end. "Why am I talking to you? It's something to do with my ankle, isn't it?" The Man in White raised his eyebrows and shrugged in a gesture that said *I'm afraid so*.

"Yes, we'd rather that wasn't the case but, that's it. I gather you've taken a bad knock on the foot, as well as a few to the old *visage*. Klaus, as you would have him be, tried to help, but he was a little slow on the ball. I think maybe he's getting old." He raised his voice when he spoke next. "You getting old, *Klausy*? Heh heh." I looked at Klaus, who was looking away from me and out of the driver's side window.

"Well, I'm hurt because of *you*. It's your fucking fault," I snapped, but there was no energy in it. I felt exhausted. The Man in White shrugged again.

"Well, if you mean the overall picture here, then yes, I can't really disagree with you," he said. "But with regard to you getting physically hurt..." He sighed and paused, as if he were choosing his next words very carefully. "There are certain protocols in place with this," he said, finally. "Things that we don't like to tell our Participants about so they can't try and *game the system,* as they say."

"What protocols?" I asked, feeling a glimmer of hope. Game the system? I could game the system? "Klaus came and helped me. That was one of them, wasn't it?" The Man in White paused for a second, his expression inscrutable behind those insect-like shades.

"Are you sure you want me to answer that?" he said. "Because I have to tell you, the protocols are actually there for your protection. If I to tell you about them, then they're cancelled. They won't apply for the reason I mentioned above. We don't like potential loopholes."

I hesitated. It was pretty obvious that Klaus *had* intervened to protect me. I didn't need that fact to be confirmed, and it was something useful to have in the back pocket... potentially. And that was the Man in White's point: if I couldn't be completely certain that Klaus would back me up in a tight spot, then I couldn't *ever* bank on it. Therefore, I couldn't *plan* to use that knowledge. And from what he was saying, it appeared that if I asked for clarification one way or another, then I would *definitely* lose Klaus' help. That was something I didn't want.

"Just tell me this then," I said, deciding on a response. "Clarify *this* because I need to know. I wasn't trying to kill anyone in the pub. Klaus helped me, fine, whatever the reason may be, you clearly know why. It could have been an attack of conscience; maybe it was a protocol; maybe he even just likes me," I couldn't resist a glance at Klaus as I said this, but he was still looking out of the window. "I don't need that clarifying, especially if it means I lose whatever potential safety net I might have. But I need to know about a different situation. Yes, I got into a fight at the pub just now, one that could have hindered my ability to complete the task. Fine. But I need to know about the actual moment when I try and kill someone. What if... what if it goes wrong... like, if I get overpowered or something... Klaus isn't allowed to help me *then*, is he? I didn't think he would but after the pub, I want to know. Just to... well, know. And I think it's only fair that you *do* tell me that. Surely telling me that doesn't change anything."

The Man in White's face went blank again. The grinning, genial tone was something that *seemed* real, and yet he had mastered the ability to just shut his face down utterly when he needed to. I remember thinking that the guy must be one hell of a poker player.

"Let me just double check whether we can tell you that, Chris," he said. "Hold on a moment, please?" The sound went dead on his end and his hand covered the camera. There was silence for about a minute. I stared dumbly at the screen. This was just *bizarre*. It was like being on the other end of my usual call centre job, except the Man in White was the one saying to me *I'd better just check with the supervisor.* I half expected him to come back on the line and say *Hello? I've got Mr. Big on the line here. He's going to take your enquiry further.* The sound kicked back in, and the Man in White's hand came away, revealing his now-grinning face once more.

"Sorry about that, Chris," he said, "I thought it'd be ok, but I just had to double check. I'm sure you understand. Yes, I can tell you the truth on that one. We don't normally announce this as it's usually not in question—and is fairly self-evident—but after what's happened today I should clarify: Klaus would *not* intervene during the process of elimination. That's on your shoulders if you screw it up, so I would choose the subject and the manner of processing very carefully in that regard. No three hundred pounders! You know what I'm saying?" he chuckled, smiling warmly.

Subject? Elimination? He sounds like he's talking about laboratory mice.

"...okay," I said.

"Good, okay. Now that's cleared up, let's get to the reason I called. Klaus tells me there's an issue with your ankle. He suspects that you've suffered some ligament damage, or possibly, a very small fracture." He stopped talking, and I realized that he was waiting for a response.

"Well... it hurts..." I said, wondering where this was going.

"Okay," the Man in White said, as if this were confirmation enough. "Well, Klaus is no doctor, but he knows well enough what to look for and we hold his judgement in the highest esteem. We take his word for it, basically. That means that you're not—for at least a few days at least—going to be operating at a reasonable capacity to do what needs to be done. And believe it or not Chris, we *do* believe in playing fair. Without going into all the details, we don't want our Participants getting hurt. That isn't the point of the exercise."

"Then what *is* the point?" I blurted out, but the Man in White held up a hand. Outside of the gloves, his fingers were thin and long.

"And *because* you have been hurt," he said, continuing as if I hadn't spoken, "it's more likely, given your current level of mobility, that it will happen again during elimination. So the good news is, for a few days at least, you're being given a time- out." He paused again, waiting, and I had nothing to say. *A time-out?* I felt a faint sense of hope that it meant I was being let off.

"Are you... does this mean it's over? I don't..." I swallowed before saying the next words, scared to say them as if the possibility of their truth might shatter if I did. "...I don't have to do it?"

The Man in White laughed, a short, genuinely amused bark.

"Ha! Oh, no, of course not! A-ha, Chris, heh heh..." He waved his hand dismissively, as if he were saying *I'm only kidding.* "No, no, of *course,* you still have to do it. You know what *time-out* means Chris! All we're doing is stopping the clock for a while."

"...oh."

It's more time. You're being given more—

"Now, of course, we will be taking the necessary steps to ensure that you aren't being given *more time*, so to speak. You know, to stop you from working on plans while in time-out, as that wouldn't be fair."

...shit.

"The initial period of time-out will be two days, well, three if you include the rest of today. Then we'll check you with some pain killers and an ankle support; see how you're doing, you know? Klaus will be the judge of the situation, and he'll decide if you need a bit longer. If it's a fracture, even a small one, you'll need a *lot* longer, but Klaus isn't sure if that's the case."

I looked at Klaus and jumped slightly in my seat when I saw that he was now staring impassively at me. I suddenly wondered how many people Klaus had witnessed being murdered. How many he'd killed himself. What would that do to someone's mind?

"Now, you'll have to surrender your phone and laptop to Klaus. You're banned from using any kind of electronic device to do any research. Obviously, we can't read your mind so you can do any planning you like in *there,* and that's the side of this that just can't be helped. But you'll remain bugged with the camera and microphone, so you can't have any conversations that sound like *planning,* Chris. Obviously, there will be a penalty in that, and the girls will have to deal with it. With me so far?"

I was. I couldn't really process his words and assess the news, but rules? Those I could at least understand. They were stopping the clock and putting things in place to prevent me from using the extra time to prepare. Well, as much as they could anyway. *Check.* Got it. Whatever you say.

"Yes. Yes, I'm with you so far."

"Ok, the other thing is that we want you to be busy. We can't have you lying around convalescing and using all that time to plan. Obviously, *that* wouldn't be fair either." The second use of the word *fair* triggered something in my head.

"*Fair?*" I shouted. "Are you fucking kidding me?" The hand came up again, but no laughter now, just solemn nodding.

"All right, all right, poor choice of words. My apologies. I meant fair to the other people who have been in your situation. *They* didn't get extra planning time."

"Fuck them!"

"Your insightful opinion aside, we want you to be busy. So, bugged and tagged and everything as I say, you'll be going into work."

"... what?"

"You'll be going into work, Chris. Into the call centre. You're not due back in until Monday anyway, but we know they're short-staffed and will be happy to have you do a Sunday shift if you call today and ask. Obviously, we'll be able to see your screen, and we can monitor it remotely even if we couldn't see it through your pin camera. We'll be able to tell if... well, I don't like to say it... if you try and tip anybody off. And as I said before, even if we suspect it... well. You know. Ok?"

I didn't say anything.

"If anybody asks what happened to your face, which I think will look a lot better by tomorrow anyway, once Christine has worked on you– "

"*Who?*"

"Well, she's not part of any protocol, but we *do* like to keep her secret until we have to," the Man in White said, making a see-saw motion with his hand. "She's our touch-up girl. We play fair Chris, as I say. Your face is a little banged up. That will bring questions, and hey, that's not something we want either."

I was stunned. A woman involved in this? Call me sexist, but the idea of a woman aiding the capture and amputation of *other innocent women* was just... is that sexist? I don't know. Somehow imagining a group of men doing all this was, and is, easier to think of. Maybe *that's* sexist.

"Does she... know?"

"Of course. We wouldn't send her otherwise."

I stared at the face on the screen. Was he wearing a wig? I supposed he could be. It would make sense.

"Who *are* you people?" I asked, finally, my voice a whisper. The grin returned, along with a gentle shake of the head.

"We *are* sorry you have to do this, Chris," he said. "but our boss is... well, he has his ways and his ideas, and we see that his wishes get carried out. Christine is a part of that. Not her real name, obviously!" he added with a chuckle.

I didn't know what to say. As I'd been doing since this whole nightmare started, my brain switched over to the logistics. Those I could deal with.

"So... when does this start?" I asked. "I mean... then that's it, until at least until the Tuesday morning time slot begins?" The Man in White pulled a face that wasn't quite a wince. It was the face the guy at the car rental place pulls when you ask about a complimentary upgrade.

"All right. Okay. Now here's the *bad* news, Chris. Again, don't shoot the messenger. But there has to be *balance* with this. Obviously, as I say, you *will* be using the extra time to think—and the whole idea of this normally is that you operate under a strict timescale of action and planning, under *pressure* as it were—but seeing as your *thinking* pressure has been reduced, there has to be, as far as the boss is concerned, a reduction on the other end of things." He stopped talking again and stared at the camera, letting it sink in. It did, but I was slow.

"No," I said. I sounded like a kid who'd been told to come in for his dinner.

"Afraid so, Chris. Afraid so."

"But I still have an hour left!" I shouted. "You've stopped the clock!"

"So you would have killed someone within the next hour? While you're barely able to walk?"

"That's not the point!"

"To be honest Chris, if you want my personal opinion," the Man in White said, scratching at his cheek, "I'd be grateful that we're stopping the clock at all, and I'd stop complaining like a little fucking bitch."

I was so shocked by the sudden change of language that my mind went blank. It had been said in the same genial tone, but I didn't know how to respond. The hand returned to his lap, and he cocked his head to one side before he spoke again, the face slack once more. "We could leave you to it and let you carry on with a non-functional foot. Meanwhile, the hours would tick by and then there'd probably be at least one girl dead and one girl a quadriplegic by the time you're able to even hobble about. *This* way, Olivia only has her arms removed, and you have a chance to get the job done before the legs and the head go—"

"*Arms?* You mean, *both* arms?"

"Yes. Better that than dead, Chris. I really wouldn't complain."

"Fuck you," I managed, and as lame as it was, somewhere inside I felt glad that at least in some small way today, I'd managed to stand up for myself. For whatever that was worth.

"Don't talk like you're doing me a favour. You bunch of lunatics are cutting innocent peoples' limbs off like they're chicken wings, and you talk like I should be *grateful!* Just stop the clock! Leave it at that!" The Man in White's hands came up to his shoulders, his *don't blame me* gesture was so high.

"No can do, Chris. Sorry," he said. He sounded like he was saying *sorry sir, the BMWs are gone, best I can do is a Kia.* "Boss's orders. He thinks it wouldn't be fair for you to get that extra time to plan and not have any consequences. I agree, but his sense of fairness is, well..." He paused, and looked at something off-camera for a moment. He smiled, and then looked back into the camera. "He's very opinionated," he said, the grin back on his face.

"*Show him to me!*" I suddenly screamed, and tried to grab the phone, but Klaus calmly shifted it to his opposite hand, placing it out of my reach. "*Put him on camera! Put him on camera!*"

"I think we're done here, Chris," the Man in White said calmly as I ranted and yelled at the phone, losing it as I knew that I'd failed and that Olivia MacArthur would never hold anything or anyone for the rest of her life, however long I managed to let that be. "Klaus will take you home. Christine will be around later to fix you up, and you'll stay there for the rest of the day. Again, you don't *have* to, and you can quit any time. Just a reminder, there. But you also know what that means. Just tell Klaus at any point if you change your mind. Oh, one thing: you may be thinking that if you hurt yourself again, or deliberately injure yourself so badly that you couldn't possibly continue with the challenge, then you'll be let off. That won't happen. That's the same as quitting. Plus, we can just wait until you heal. I said that one should be in the initial rules, but it wasn't agreed. After today, it was decided that you should know that."

"Don't you hang up on me!"

"I'm done here, Klaus," the Man in White said, and Klaus turned the phone over to end the call. The phone went back in Klaus' jacket, he fastened his seatbelt, and then turned the key in the ignition as I tensed my entire body in my seat and let out a primal scream of frustration. The car pulled away, and the Man in White's words danced around in my head like a needle just out of reach of an addict.

You can quit any time. You can quit any time.

I could. I knew I could. That was the worst part. I was *choosing* to stay a part of this... and yet I didn't have any choice at all.

And now I was going home. To wait for Christine.

***

THE SECOND DAY OF THE TIME-OUT, MONDAY MORNING:

Harry's back is already up when he sees Chris. And it wouldn't cause such a reaction, today of all days, if Chris wasn't one of the slackers. If he was someone who had shown any real dedication to the job. But Chris is one of the young slackers, and it's already been a bad day for Harry.

Those damn cats had started it off by keeping him awake all night. Then, at breakfast, Ruth had spilt orange juice all over his shirt as they'd both bustled around the kitchen. Fine, no big deal, an accident, but instead of apologizing she'd shouted at him and called him an idiot. That had led to an upstairs-to-downstairs screaming match as he'd gone for a shirt replacement, a verbal war of attrition that had lasted until he stormed out the door, leaving his briefcase in the hallway. He'd had to go back for it, making him twenty minutes late. Then he'd arrived at work to find out that Linda was sick and that he had to manage not just his team, but hers, and this during the week that he was supposed to be preparing the stat report to the upper-level brass. All of that together has meant that he's tired, he's angry, and he's stressed.

And here's Chris, in the wrong place at the wrong time.

Harry doesn't expect the world from the call centre kids. He knows it's a temp call centre job for most of them. They're here for beer money, clearing student debt, or making funds to get them through until Christmas. They're doing the bare minimum and going home, and they're not here to start a career in customer service. Harry gets it, and he gets it because he was the same as them once, at least in terms of age. Harry never went to university, and anyone that ever says he has a chip on his shoulder towards the younger staff because of that – and a few people have, never to his face but he knows they have – is just plain wrong. Harry would never be jealous towards the younger team members because he has what they never will: street smarts. *You can't get* that *shit from a book, oh no.*

To be fair, most of them, at least, are on time. Most of them, at least, make a reasonable effort. Ok, there's always something Harry has to pick up on now and then (and he does, Harry runs a tight ship, and again, anyone that says he nitpicks is simply a slacker, another one of those cocksuckers that are never going to go as far as he has), and yes, he has to explain to them how he got where he is through a good work ethic and observing the rules. *But of course, Harry gets what these kids are about. And it certainly doesn't hurt to have some eye candy about. What was that line?* I keep getting older but college girls stay the same age. *Ruth is certainly getting older too, but not the young staff, especially the student staff. That's a perk, for sure. He'd never* do *anything, but it doesn't hurt to look. And a little flirting is harmless too. He knows they enjoy it, anyway.*

But Chris has been one of the worst offenders. And he isn't even a student! This is his full-time job! *Shouldn't that be worth* something? *Always a minute or two late. Arrival time is 8:30 am, not 8:31, not 8:32. If you're not five minutes early, you're late. That's one of* Harry's Rules, *for certain, probably his number one.*

Harry has caught Chris texting in the past when he was supposedly listening to customers. That was a dressing down, and yes, Harry had done it in front of everyone else and some *would say that was a bit much, but Harry has to make examples. Harry has caught Chris eating at his station, which other supervisors (the ones with no goddamn ambition, that's for sure) might let slide. But in Harry's book, the rules are the rules, and if he's caught letting his staff break them then it's* his *balls that get busted. The kid's attitude to work is just* slack. *Sure, his call completion rate is high, and when the customers accept the feedback texts they rate him highly too. But it's an* attitude *thing, Harry knows, even if other people don't see it. And Harry always sees that shit. Fair enough, the kid even asked to come in an extra day, and that had been a Sunday no less, but so what? The kid just needs the extra money; that doesn't make* him *dedicated.*

Harry's never had to sack a kid Chris' age, but he has had to give a few bollockings. After the last two days—especially after the day that Harry has had so far—Chris is about to get a very big bollocking indeed.

Yesterday had been bad enough. The kid was clearly hungover, coming into work looking like a total mess. Limping as well, perhaps because of a fight the night before? Yes, it's a call centre, and no, the customers on the phones don't actually see the employees, but Harry runs a tight ship. *He just doesn't like it. If Harry hadn't been rushed off his feet yesterday, he'd have already said something. All through Sunday, he'd kept seeing Chris with his head in his hands or rubbing at his eyes, nodding at whatever the customer in his headset was saying. Harry had checked: Chris' call* completion rate was down eleven percent. Just unacceptable. If it hadn't been for the fact that Harry had a meeting with marketing yesterday that went on for most of the afternoon, Harry would have given Chris one of his famous dressing downs. The kid had gotten away with it.

But then it had happened again today. Chris had come in looking like death warmed up. And now, as Harry is making his way back to his office, he sees Chris rubbing at his eyes, his headset off his head.

Chris has picked the wrong day to slack. This is going to be biblical.

"Chris!" Harry shouts—he makes sure to shout it, feeling a grim thud of satisfaction as several heads pop up to observe what's going to happen—as he storms over to Chris' station. Chris jumps in his seat and turns to look at Harry as he descends upon him. Yep, the kid's eyes are bloodshot, with heavy dark circles under them. Harry would never allow himself to be seen at work like that. Once he's close enough to be within earshot of the customer on the line, Harry goes into miming mode. He thrusts a finger at the headset and pantomimes jamming it onto his own head. Chris nods, pale and blinking, and puts it on. Harry stands with his arms folded, staring daggers, while Chris finishes with the customer's request to book a callout for tomorrow morning (although the earliest Chris can give her, as a non-priority customer, i.e. no one elderly in the home and with the boiler situation not being an emergency, is next

Wednesday). Out of the corners of his eyes, Harry can see more and more headsetted people taking notice, waiting for Chris to finish the call. Perfect.

Chris finishes, having set his system to Away *to prevent the next call from automatically coming on the line—usually only reserved for sanctioned breaks under Harry's watch, but the kid clearly knows what's coming, and that's good—and removes his headset, swiveling his chair around to face Harry fully. Harry crooks his finger at Chris, as if he were summoning a dog. It's such an obvious but seldom-used trick to establish power, and Harry can't believe more people don't do it. He'd read it in a book about dominance assertion. Chris pauses for a second and then stands, head down. Harry walks a few feet away to give the illusion of taking the conversation out of earshot of the nearby stations, but actually still close enough that everyone in his section will hear everything. Chris slowly limps his way over.*

"Sorry... Harry," Chris says, and he sounds like he's about to fall asleep. "I just, uh... I have a headache. It's really bad. I won't let that happen again."

"Did I just see that right?" says Harry, loud enough for everyone to hear.

"Er... well, I—"

"Did you just keep a customer waiting? Was the customer talking to someone who wasn't listening?"

"I'm really sorry Harry, but I only asked her to hold on a second— "

"Hold on a second?" Harry cries. That was pushing it; that might have been heard by the customers currently on the lines, but the example has to be made and now everyone nearby is listening. Still working, of course—Harry wouldn't allow that to stop—but with one ear on Harry. "Customers don't have a second, Chris. They're busy people. What would you say if you went to the hospital, bleeding to death, and they told you to hang on a second?" *Chris blinks in response, and Harry suddenly has the flash that he gets sometimes. He's realized that he's said something a little stupid, or something slightly over the top, and for the briefest of nanoseconds he's back in the playground at fifteen-years-old, and Simon Paulson and Terry Billingley are leading the others in the usual point-and-jeer fest and leaving Harry feeling very, very exposed. Harry bites it back as always—he's very good at that these days and has been for years—and moves past it the best way he knows. "Something smart to say about that, Chris? Let's hear it." The kid stares at Harry for a moment with those tired, clearly hungover eyes, and then shakes his head.*

"No, Harry. You're absolutely right. I'm really sorry. I've not been sleeping well. I'm sorry."

"What you do on your own time is your business, but when it affects your work it's my *business, Chris."*

"Absolutely. That's, uh... that's totally understandable."

This isn't getting the response Harry wanted. The kid is just agreeing.

"You look a mess," Harry snaps, pushing away the pent-up anger from the morning (and a lot of other times at home recently, now that he thinks about it, he pushes that away too). "Clean yourself up before tomorrow." He's getting angrier, and he doesn't know why. He wants a reaction *from the little shit. Harry lowers his voice a touch, as this zinger could get him in trouble, but if no one else hears it but him and the kid it's Chris' word against his. "If you're out on the booze trying to get fucking laid, you might want to tidy yourself up. Then maybe you might get a look in for once. You look a* mess." *Boom. Harry holds back a smirk—giving the kid some home truths that should bring him down a peg or two, and Chris really* does *look a mess—but for some reason, the kid just blinks a few times.*

Then those tired eyes, carrying a gaze that had previously been frantically trying to look anywhere but at Harry, slowly come up and settle on Harry's face. The kid's brow furrows slightly, and he doesn't say anything. Harry has the flash again and that makes him even angrier. What is this fuckup thinking?

"You're agency staff, Chris," *Harry growls.* "I can get rid of your slobby face anytime I like, so I'd choose my next words very carefully if I were you, son." Son *is pushing it; Harry is only twenty-eight, not a lot older than Chris, but he's a damn sight wiser, that's for sure.*

"I wasn't drinking last night, Harry," Chris says, and his voice is a lot calmer all of a sudden. His eyes don't leave Harry's. *"Or the night before. I just haven't been sleeping. I have a lot of... personal stuff going on."*

"I don't give a shit, Chris," Harry says quietly, and he means it. *"You can...."* Then Harry notices something. A little strange spot right by Chris' eye, one that, once clocked, reveals similar strangeness around Chris' face, especially on his nose. It's like a Magic Eye picture, once you can see edge the whole thing just leaps out at you. A slow smirk begins to spread across Harry's face. *"Are you... are you wearing* makeup, *Chris?"* The smirk gets bigger as Chris's steady gaze finally cracks and his eyes begin to dart around again. *"You are, aren't you?"*

In a distant part of his brain – one that even Harry probably doesn't realize exists – Harry suddenly begins to feel like Simon Paulson and Terry Billingley. The smirk becomes a grin. *"Is that something you wear to make you look better? When you go out?"* He's going too far, and he knows it, way too far, but his voice is low now—the observers have lost interest—and he has decided that he's going to get rid of this fucking kid, understaffed or not. Doing so would make him feel a hell of a lot better than he has for days. He might as well enjoy it. Chris' head drops, and Harry feels so powerful that he almost feels ashamed. Almost.

He waits. Chris' head doesn't come up. Harry savours the moment. As soon as he looks up again, Harry is going to tell him that he's—

"Harry," Chris *says, without looking up, "Can I tell you something? Something that I haven't told anyone else?" It sounds like he's going to say* go fuck yourself *or something, and Harry opens his mouth to say* you're fired *before Chris can say it because that would mean Chris was quitting by choice, and* that *would mean that Chris would win. But Chris gets there first. "Because I need some advice, Harry. And I know you've had to bollock me a few times, but I think that you're a pretty worldly-wise guy. Even if we don't always see eye-to-eye, I could really do with your opinion." Chris' head comes up and the gaze is steady again... but different. Harry actually shrinks back slightly, catches himself. Why does he feel unsettled? But then the kid makes it better by saying:*

"You've made a success of yourself. You've overcome adversity, I'm sure. I just need, you know... some advice. From an older guy. A successful older guy."

In his total surprise, Harry feels his anger drain away, as if someone has pulled a plug somewhere in his brain. The effect is so relaxing, and the tension drains out of his shoulders as his mind fills with something else: his ego. Well, well, well. This is a turnup for the books. Maybe the kid can be kicked into line after all. Harry almost visibly swells, his stupidity rendering him utterly unable to see when he is being so obviously played.

"You want to sort your shit out, do you?" Harry mutters, nodding and smirking. *"I can't say it's not overdue, Chris."* A flash of what Harry believes to be compassion skims across his forebrain. *"And look, if you have stuff going on that's affecting your work, that's my business too. If you want to tell me, I'm all ears."* He doesn't actually give a shit, but it feels good to say that he does. He likes the idea of a mentor role.

"Can we talk somewhere else?" Chris says. His voice is very flat and steady. *"I'm due for a lunch break now anyway. I don't want to talk here."*

"Hmm, well I'm very busy, but I can spare five minutes," Harry says, already regretting the offer as he says it. But it might get the little twat in line, so...

"How about we go down to the smoking area?" Chris says quietly, very quietly. *"I don't smoke, but you know, the smoking area would be ideal. It would be perfect, in fact. Quiet. And I don't want to talk about personal stuff in here, you know, in the workplace. Can we go now?"* He pauses. *"I want to... I want to get this done before I change my mind."*

Harry looks at Chris for a moment, amused almost.

"Sure," he says, finally. *"Let's go."* He walks ahead of Chris, chuckling to himself and shaking his head a little. Somehow, this is actually making him feel a lot better.

He doesn't see Chris pause at his desk and pick up a pencil. Doesn't see him roll it into his fist, three inches of pointed wood *sticking out. Chris then hurries to catch up with the now-striding Harry. Harry likes to stride.*

They emerge into the slightly windy outdoors, protected from it by the bus shelter-like plastic windbreak that covers the front of the smoking area. It's noisy out here; the call centre is the building furthest north in the industrial park. That means it's closest to the motorway that buzzes constantly away to the left, hidden behind the high hedge that conceals it. There are two or three other people in the smoking area, a girl and two men, apparently relative strangers, a fact clarified by the distance between them all. Harry rubs at his exposed arms, his short-sleeved shirt—of course— adorned Sipowicz-style with a tie.

"Bloody November," he mutters. He's right. The sun isn't out, and the breeze is making the air chilled, if not outright cold. He looks at Chris, waiting, but Chris is looking at the other people in the smoking area. The kid then steps closer to Harry, leaning in conspiratorially. He's back to not making eye contact.

"Yeah..." he says, tutting in a way that Harry isn't sure is exactly genuine, "I thought this might be the case. There are too many people here. I don't really want this to be overheard. Can we go over behind the drum shed?" He gestures over his shoulder with his head. He doesn't need to, Harry knows where it is; around the side of the building, a few feet shy of the hedge. It isn't used anymore, apart from the few workers that ride to work who store their bikes in there. Many years ago, in the call centre's previous life

as a print works, the used industrial drums were stored in there until collection.

Harry's internal logic does a little dance, giving him an answer that he doesn't fully believe. The makeup, going behind the drum shed... is the kid going to confess that he's a faggot? He's going to come out to Harry? Surely not. Not Harry of all people. The kid says he just wants advice. Harry doesn't have a problem with faggots; he just doesn't really know what to do around them (not that he's ever really met many). No, that's a silly thought, even though he always thought the kid could be a faggot. Either way, the reassurance that he's given himself gives him a sense of relief, and all of a sudden he just wants this over with so he can get on with things again. What is he doing out here anyway? This was stupid. He needs to get back inside.

"Yes, yes, whatever Chris, but the clock is ticking, I don't have long." They start to walk. "I want to help and everything, but, you know, we're short-staffed, and I've got a lot to do."

"That's fine, I understand," says Chris, his voice flat and leaden again. Is it drugs, Harry wonders? That would explain a lot. He notices Chris looking up at the side of the building, high up into the very edges of the structure. There are no windows on this side, just a concrete wall. He absent-mindedly follows Chris' gaze, not really noticing anything, especially not the cameras that only face away from them to cover the fire exit fifty feet away.

They reach the far side of the drum shed and Chris turns to face Harry. Harry is a little taller, so Chris is looking up into his eyes slightly, and Harry wonders if it's the light or the angle or the tiredness in them but geez, *in that moment the kid barely looks human.*

"Spit it out then Chris, no one here," Harry says, beginning to get annoyed again. How the hell was he down here? He'd let the kid appeal to his ego, he realizes. He let that happen sometimes. He'll give Chris a minute. "What is it, bud?" Harry always uses 'bud" when he's trying to come across as pally. "Job interview? Career choice? I just have to be quick." Chris doesn't say anything and continues to stare at Harry, and Harry notices how Chris is thumbing the sharpened tip of the pencil that he's gripping in his right hand. It's almost a nervous gesture.

"Well?" Harry asks.

"I'd like to quit this job, Harry," Chris says eventually. His gaze is locked on once more, laser-focused on Harry's eyes. "But I can't. I have to live a normal life."

Harry snorts, shaking his head.

"That's the difference between you and me, Chris," Harry says. "Between you and me and the rest of your lot. You see a job, and you just think about how you want to quit, but boo-hoo, you don't have a choice. Now me, I see a job, and even if I don't like it, I think, 'where's the opportunity? What good can I get out of this?' If your lot spent as much time thinking about the positives as they do

whining, you'd all do a lot better." Harry shakes his head again. This was it? Pathetic. He doesn't think about how much he complains to Ruth about getting constantly looked over for promotion, and certainly *doesn't think about how this may be due to him ignoring the many adjustments the higher-ups have asked him to make to his management style. After all,* those *idiots know* nothing.

"You're absolutely right, Harry," Chris says, his lips then pressing tightly together as he nods solemnly. Chris cocks his head to one side. "I think you're absolutely right. I think I've thought about some good that can come out of this workplace right now."

"Well, good," says Harry, looking at his watch. This was a total waste of time. Chris' lot are all the same, he knows; good at saying they'll make changes, but never doing it. "Then maybe you—"

"Hold on one more minute please, Harry," Chris says, holding up a finger, and to Harry's mild surprise, Chris then walks around to Harry's other side. He stands far enough away for Harry not to fully realize it, but Chris is now standing in Harry's way, right between Harry and the path back to the smoking area. "I just want to... double check one more thing. Do you... do you have children?"

"No," Harry says immediately, so surprised by the question that he answers it without thinking. "Why?"

Chris just stares at Harry in response, but he starts blinking very rapidly. Chris starts to breathe a bit more heavily too. Harry wonders if the kid is about to start crying, but no tears come. And *then Chris' jaw sets, and his head starts to tremble a bit, and Harry thinks that Chris is going to hit him. He's suddenly sure of it.*

The hairs go up on Harry's neck, and he freezes. He's never been in a fight in his life, and although Chris is shorter, he must weigh the same as Harry. Has Chris been in fights? Is he a fighter? Harry begins to panic on the inside, thinking about pulling rank, but to do that would be to acknowledge that he thinks Chris is going to hit him and if he does that and he's wrong and Chris wasn't going to then Chris would know that Harry thought it and then everyone in the office would know and then—

Harry looks at the pencil in Chris' hand. Chris' thumb is pressed down so hard against the point now that blood is running down its shaft. Harry goes cold and just about pisses his pants.

"Chris—"

Chris then blinks again, and looks down at the pencil like he'd forgotten it was there. He stares at it for a moment.

"Oh," he says in a cracked voice, and now he does *sound like he's on the verge of tears. "Would you look at that?" He sounds like a robot, entirely devoid of emotion, yet his demeanor is as if he could shatter at any minute. "I sharpened it too much." Suddenly, Chris spins on the spot, and in an incredibly violent movement he flings the pencil over the hedge, spittle flying from his lips as his head whips round with the throw. Harry flinches as this happens, but immediately composes himself afterwards before Chris can turn around.*

"Thanks for the advice, Harry," Chris says in that same horrible robot voice, without turning around. "I really appreciate it. I'm gonna grab some food now. The stuff you saw today won't happen again. I promise."

Then Chris walks away, back towards the call centre.

Harry watches him go and realizes just how fast his breath is, how much he's trembling. What the fuck was that? The kid is fucking crazy!

Harry spends the next ten minutes behind the shed, rationalizing, and reassuring. Harry is very good at that. By the time he's done, he's not only convinced himself that he had the situation under control, but that he actually gave the kid some sound life advice.

But somewhere in his subconscious, a mental note is made: cut the kid some slack.

***

Christine hadn't been what I'd expected.

If I'm honest, I guess I'd imagined some evil but alluring femme fatale, all cheekbones and high heels and elbow gloves. But she wasn't at all. She was wearing the obligatory sunglasses of course, along with a baseball cap, but she was about 5'2" and I'd guess her age as being around 50. She didn't speak when she arrived— Klaus pointed to tell me to let her in, and he followed me to the door—except to say hello and instruct me to sit and turn my head at the relevant points. She didn't even talk to Klaus. She said, "please Chris" after every instruction—*chin up please Chris, close your eyes please, Chris, close your mouth please, Chris*—which I think might have been a way of appearing respectful, but I didn't like it. I didn't like her using my name.

"Why are you working with these people?" I asked her at one point. "Are they making you do it? How long have you been doing this?"

She stopped her rummaging in her bag of tricks and looked at me for a moment.

"Do you want people to ask questions when you go to work?" she asked. Her voice was sweet, like a nice schoolteacher in a kid's TV show. "You look like you've been beaten up, Chris. People don't let other people brush that off. They might *not* ask questions, but they probably will. And you know what that could cause. However slim the chance, do you want to risk that?" Another bug-eyed face, staring straight at me. I wondered what Klaus would do if I slapped her. Maybe nothing. Maybe something. Maybe she knew a few Klaus-moves of her own.

"No," I said.

"Then let me finish what I'm doing and I'll be out of your hair."

Out of your hair. As if she were apologising for vacuuming around my feet or something.

By the time she was finished, you would never be able to tell that anything had happened unless you were as familiar as I was with how my nose should look. She said that it would last until after work tomorrow as long as I didn't wash it and that she'd be back the next night to do a touch-up.

Then she left, and after I had called HR at the call centre—who were indeed delighted to hear that I could come and do an extra Sunday shift if I were needed, which of course I was—I looked at Klaus.

"Now what?" I said, but there was no anger in it. I was empty. "We just... we wait?" Klaus nodded in response, then picked up the remote and turned on the TV. Some nondescript midday show was on, but Klaus began to turn the volume up as if he were interested. Then, as the volume began to reach earsplitting levels, I realized what he was doing. He handed the remote to me, gestured at the TV—*watch what you want,* the wave of the hand said—and sat down in the armchair opposite. His eyes were on me.

"This isn't necessary," I yelled over the din of the TV. *"I'm out of ideas. You don't have to keep me distracted."* I didn't know if that was true—I had no idea what my next move would be, and whether or not I was capable of coming up with something that I could live with—but I just wanted him to turn the damn thing *down.* I had no idea that our TV could even *be* that loud. Klaus shrugged in response, of course. *"I can quit,"* I shouted, but not in

anger. *"I can quit at any time and you'd have to leave."* Klaus nodded again. *It's all the same to me,* the nod said. *I just work here, kid.*

I looked back at the screen and knew there was no way I was going to quit. Because I knew in that moment, as I sat in my comfortable chair listening to the uncomfortable racket from the TV, that Olivia was having both of her arms amputated. You might think that would spur me into thought, a driving force to fire brain cells and neurons and whatever cunning I had left into a eureka moment ... but it didn't. It had the opposite effect. It paralysed me. Not to mention the questions that screamed and bellowed in my head even louder than the TV's speakers.

How will they do it? Will they use a chainsaw? Surely not, not even them. A circular surgeon's saw maybe? Would they cauterize the wound? How do you cauterize a wound that big? It would have to come off at the shoulder; that's a big hole. Would they cut below the shoulder? Halfway up the arm, or just below the shoulder, like a Greek statue?

I bit down mentally, and decided that finding something to watch—for now at least—would be a good idea. Something to help me switch off. The "time out" was on at least until Tuesday morning anyway, and so maybe getting my mind off it would actually help relieve some pressure and let me think clearly. *Yeah, that's it,* I told myself, trying desperately to ignore the knowledge that I'd failed.

Klaus followed me around the house, watching me make food that I ended up not even touching. He watched me sleep, or rather, watched me try to sleep that night. When I finally did—and extremely briefly at that—I had terrible dreams that I don't want to revisit here. I watched the ceiling of my room turn from black to dark blue to grey to its actual white. By the time I made it into work the next morning, dropped off by Klaus who remained in the car with his surveillance gear—*didn't the man ever eat*, I wondered, *unless he has astronaut food or something inside those endless pockets of his*—I was hobbling through the door like a corpse. I didn't speak to anyone any more than to say "hi" and kept my head down so as to avoid any dealings with Harry the Twat.

I barely heard a word any of the customers said. Fortunately, so much of it was stuff that I could do on autopilot that I was able to blag my way through the day. *Un*fortunately, the Man in White and his friends were right; it was near impossible to keep my head on the real task at hand. Exhaustion, stress, constant distraction, and pain all combined to make planning next to impossible.

To my disgust, dear unknown reader who will probably never fucking read this anyway, that was almost fine by me. I was running away from it.

Then something happened, despite the best intentions of the Man in White. Or maybe this was what he wanted all along. I don't know.

Out of nowhere, I had an idea.

A horrible, horrible idea. A eureka moment in the darkness.

It came with a creeping, dawning dread that began to work its way into my brain as the day wore on. I tried to ignore it—of course I did—but as the other options were looked at, examined, and dismissed, it became harder and harder to ignore. It couldn't be true. It couldn't.

But it rang a bell, no, a *fire station bell* in a way that *drug dealer* or *racist* – the only targets I could actually find – hadn't. It *screamed* truth.

I got through the day and Klaus drove me home to await Christine. She actually said *hiya* when I opened the door, using the same sing-song tone a personal and familiar masseuse might use when she came around for the weekly back rub. I didn't say anything and let her in.

Halfway through the touch-up, it all became too much, and I ran to the toilet to throw up. Klaus ran after me, of course. When I came back, Christine tutted and reworked around my mouth.

It can't be true. I thought it over and over again, even though it made no difference.

There was still a whole extra day left in the time-out. Inspiration would come, I knew. *Another* idea. Salvation, a way out. I hobbled up the stairs at 8 pm, Ibuprofen running through my veins. I desperately needed to sleep. Klaus followed me like an attentive lover hoping for action.

Sleep didn't come. The thoughts did. The knowledge did. I knew—but somehow wouldn't accept—that I was merely prolonging the inevitable. It was like a boot made of lead repeatedly kicking me in the brain, a near-fact that smashed into my mind.

It'll be all right, I thought, desperate in the darkness. *There'll be another way. Something will happen tomorrow and you'll know what it is.*

It was a pointless thought, a lit match trying to withstand a toxic dam that had burst its banks.

The funny thing was that—now I was running freely from my thoughts rather than wrestling them into order—my mind was totally blank. I went into work, running not just my job but myself on autopilot too. Even so, as the hours went by, the truth became louder and louder and louder and louder and louder and louder and louder.

A woman on the phone said her name was Olivia, and I nearly lost it. I half expected the next words out of her mouth to be *help us.* I broke from the call and got into an altercation with my boss that I won't go into here. Let's just say I was dazed, delirious, and very nearly ended my role as a Participant at his expense.

But I didn't. He's an asshole, but he didn't deserve to die.

That was the problem, don't you see? Despite any offhand jokes you might make; despite the fact that someone can piss you off so much that you're practically foaming at the mouth; despite the fact that you will run into a minimum of one person a month who will absolutely stagger you with sheer selfishness or arrogance or unkindness or stupidity or all of the above... very, very, *very* few people *deserve* to die. And even for those that do: what are the odds of them being around you, being able to be found, *and* displaying the very reason they need to die *right in front of you?*

That was why, when Klaus pulled the car up outside my house after work towards the end of the second day of time-out, I put my hand on his arm as he began to get out of the car.

"Wait," I said. Klaus slowly turned to me, looking mildly surprised, a fact that was somehow clear even through his shades. "Wait a second." I looked at my fingers on his arm. They were shaking. I felt like I couldn't breathe.

There has to be another way, a voice said for the millionth time. Then another one spoke up, one I hadn't heard before, and it came with a certainty that I have come to doubt in the years since. When the nights become so like those nights in the time-out that I sometimes lurch upright in my bed and expect to see Klaus sitting in the corner, an unmoving and watchful troll dimly illuminated by the half-light of the early morning. I think about that voice, and

I *know it was the only way...* but then I suddenly don't and it never, ever ends.

Maybe there is, the voice said. *But this is the only option that* you *can take, Chris.*

"I want to speak to the Man in White," I said, quietly. "I want to ask him something."

***

Part Three: Closing

"Oh God, what have I done?" - Ben Folds

Chapter Six: A Radical New Approach, A Transitional Period, and A Relocation Package

***

I told you at the start that I began this journal as a way of trying to truly purge the crap inside of me. To try and at least put down *some* of the bags of rocks that I've been carrying around. And that's true, to an extent. I'll never be able to put them all down, I know that, but that's not what I mean. I mean there's another reason why I finally did this. Why I stopped thinking about it after all of these years and actually did it, actually wrote it.

The Man in White came to see me again a week ago.

***

After telling Klaus that I needed to speak to the Man in White, he'd started tapping away on that phone of his once more. It took a long time for anyone to arrive.

I remember watching the clock and experiencing the most agonizing fucking wait of my life. I thought I would go mad. I can't describe it, so I'm not going to try. I just need you to understand that... look, I'm going to try to stick to the facts—it will be easier that way, and this is very, very hard for me to even begin to talk about—so if I sound in any way cold and robotic, I wasn't. It was the worst night of my life.

Eventually, I jumped out of my armchair—Klaus seated in his now-predictable spot in the chair opposite—at the sound of two cars' tyres crunching on the gravel in the driveway. I hobbled to the window and looked out. It was so late now that the sun had very nearly disappeared; the shadows of the two black Range Rovers that were now parked outside cast into lengthy shapes, darker stretches that crossed the entire yard in the fading light. Both vehicles had blacked-out windows. Something told me that I would be completely wasting my time memorizing the cars' plates.

As I looked, eight men of various shapes, colours, and sizes stepped out of the Range Rovers. All of them were dressed similarly to Klaus: sunglasses, big coats, and gloves. None were as large as Klaus, though. I looked at him and saw that he was already standing. He held out a hand towards the door. *After you.*

I swallowed. I began to limp towards the front door of the house, and to my surprise, Klaus put out a hand to support my shoulder. I looked up at him, but he was looking straight ahead. We walked to the front door, and I opened it.

I had never known the immediate outside of my house to be as silent as it was that evening. The weather, with weirdly inverse timing, was warm for the time of year. The men that gathered outside stared at me like my own strange personal collection of hitmen statues.

One of them stepped back from the rear door of the right-hand Range Rover, still holding on to it with one arm. The request was obvious, and I began to move towards it, Klaus alongside me. The men's heads turned as I passed, their bodies stationary. It was just fucking *bizarre* in the silence. Then the man holding the door turned to me as I drew close and held out a hand. I'd been prepped for this, so I spread my arms and legs. The man patted me down, rifled through my pockets, and then nodded, satisfied. He stepped back and gestured to the car once more.

Klaus steadied me as I pushed with my good leg and clambered up onto the leather-upholstered back seat. One of the men moved to follow in after me, but Klaus held up a finger without looking at him. The man stopped, paused for a moment, then stepped back slightly. Klaus moved into the car after me and settled into the seat to my right. I didn't know whether to be flattered or worried. The rest of the car's seats filled up, and I could see the opposite vehicle was already full of large men.

As the engine started, something tapped against my chest. I looked down to see Klaus' hand holding an eye mask, the type you see people using on planes when they want to sleep. I took it without question – although I did take a second to wonder if there was anything Klaus *didn't* have in his goddamn pockets - and began to put it on. I hesitated as I caught sight of my front door through the Range Rover's windscreen. For the briefest moment, I could imagine my parents inside, watching TV or arguing in the kitchen, maybe Mum working in the garden or Dad at the kitchen table doing the Times crossword.

My hands felt numb as I put the mask on. Once it was in place, I felt gloved hands sealing the bottom edge of the mask to my face with some kind of tape. I felt the Range Rover move backwards and then my journey began, sandwiched tightly between two killers in the back seat.

It went on for fucking hours.

I don't know if it was because our destination actually was that far away or whether they just drove around and around to make me completely lose my bearings (I couldn't have tracked our movements anyway if I tried), but all I know is that I was nearly insane with anxiety and boredom by the time I heard the handbrake go on. It would have been bad enough—all that time in silence surrounded by lunatics—but doing so blindfold made it an eternity.

I felt the pressure ease off either of my long-suffering shoulders as Klaus and the other man opposite me disembarked from the car. I sat still, awaiting instructions that I knew would come, and I wasn't disappointed.

"Hi, Chris." I knew that voice. My skin crawled. I could hear the smile in it. "Just a little further now, okay? Bounce on over to the edge of the seat and we'll help you get down."

I did as I was told, and felt gloved hands take my shoulders. I was slowly guided down to terra firma, and even my young legs cried out slightly as I finally stretched them after all that time in the back seat. My injured ankle did a little extra crying out of its own. It had recovered slightly in the last two days, but not by much. I suspected it was a slight fracture, after all, a fact that I had confirmed not long after all of this.

"You okay?" The Man in White said, making me jump. He sounded like he was right by my ear.

"Of course not," I said, doing a bad job of hiding how much he'd startled me. "Let's just..." I realized that this was it. *Let's just get on with it* did it no justice whatsoever. I didn't finish my sentence.

"Yes, let's," the Man in White said, and the utterly false somberness in his voice made me want to throw up. Two sets of hands gently steered me, and we began to walk slowly, my guides perhaps being careful of my injury. I found myself appreciating it. The ground beneath my feet had give to it; grass. I simultaneously realized how quiet it was, and not just because it was, by now, so late. We were in the middle of nowhere, even by the standards of my own home's semi-rural surroundings. This was something altogether different. *Full*-rural.

"Where are we?" I asked, quietly. The question was automatic and stupid. The Man in White gave me a pass by not scoffing.

"Where you wanted to go, of course," he said. I couldn't read the tone this time. "Step up," he added, and I heard a door open. The pace we were walking at slowed for a moment, and I knew this was the point at which I had to lift my good foot. It came down on something more solid, and I knew that we'd entered some kind of building. As we moved forward, I noticed how much cooler it was inside wherever we were, and then I heard the door we'd entered through close behind us. I nearly panicked, hearing only ten sets of footsteps and the breath of men I didn't know. Strangers who were capable of being a part of something like this.

I heard another door open. This one was definitely heavier; the lock scraped hugely and then clanged, and as it swung open I could feel a change in the air and heard a distinct sound of *pulling*, like the seal on a fire door coming apart but louder. Even from here, the change in air pressure told me that the room beyond was much, much larger than the one through which we'd entered.

I felt those same gloved hands pull the tape free from the mask, then the mask itself was removed. Before I could catch a glimpse through the large doorway in front of me, something else went over my entire head, but I could still see clearly. I felt wool on my cheeks, a snugness enveloping my head.

A ski mask. Just like I'd requested.

We stepped through the doorway, and I took in my surroundings. This room was bright. Several new people were standing around—maybe five or six, I can't remember—all dressed similarly to Klaus. Suits. Black ties. Sunglasses too of course, and all were pointing at me.

Strip lighting adorned the high ceiling. The walls were made of brick and looked old. The flooring looked new: black linoleum. Despite the age of the walls, the place looked as if it had been scrubbed clean. Against one wall there was a row of computers, most of which were currently off, with an array of headsets and what I guessed were surveillance devices of some kind. There was a faint hum of air conditioning and processor banks.

At the other end of the room was something else. Someone else.

The train of thought had been steady, as I told you earlier, and had all started with a simple realization that had settled into my brain when I was at work; it had become self-evident and undeniable. Had it not been for the time-out, I think I would have bumbled through the whole Process not knowing the truth until it was too late.

But we *did* have the time-out, and I *did* realize.

I hadn't let Neil live because he wasn't that bad of a person. I hadn't let the arsehole in the Bonny Minstrel live because he was a parent. Yes, they were part of the reason, but they were also excuses that stopped me from seeing the real truth. And it was a very simple truth.

The rules the Man in White and Co. had laid out were *perfect.* No suicides. No one elderly. No one with a terminal illness. At least, those rules were perfect for *me,* in so much as they meant I couldn't operate within the system. That's what I realized.

I realized that I simply couldn't kill anyone who didn't want to die. Someone with the rest of their lives ahead of them. I couldn't take it away.

I didn't have it in me.

That had been the first realization.

And then another one had come, and with it, a horrible, horrible solution.

At the far end of the room—more of a hall, to describe it properly—were a row of large booths. No, that doesn't do them justice. They were more like tiny *rooms,* each of them shed-sized and made of concrete with a large, heavy-looking single door and a big plexiglass window at the front. These were lined up against the far wall. They were around ten feet square, certainly large enough to house a single bed, and of course, each of them did just that. Each booth-room had a metal box of some sort that passed through the roof, and into those boxes ran a large duct that disappeared into the hall's ceiling. I guessed they must have been supplying oxygen and extracting carbon dioxide. Or maybe it was just air conditioning. Either way, I assumed all *that* because the sheds were somehow completely soundproof. I knew *this* part because I couldn't clearly hear even one of the words that were being screamed on the inside.

Each bed contained a girl, and each girl was one I recognized. They were shackled to the bed by what looked like some kind of soft leather restraints around their legs and wrists, except of course for the girl inside the first booth in the row. She didn't have any wrists to restrain. She was bound by her legs and her neck.

The second realization of the time-out had been blindingly obvious. The rules meant, for me at least, that anyone I could have justified killing—the suicides, the nearly-dead, the going-to-die-from-illnesses—were off-limits. A great big Magic Because taken away as an option. And sitting at my call centre station, I had wished and wished that I could see the future. That I could somehow *know* how and when someone was going to die, that I could magically identify someone that was *already* a dead man walking. If, by some stroke of extreme luck, I suddenly developed this power of prophecy, then I could then simply step in ahead of time, guilt-free, and save the five girls by taking out that already-doomed person a little bit earlier. I sat at my desk and imagined all of the many ways this impossible scenario could play out... and in that moment of pointless dark whimsy, I had my answer. My Magic Because.

I knew exactly where a dead *woman* walking could be found.

And I could save her four sisters in the process.

On the other side of her shed-booth's window, Olivia's arms were bandaged, and she was the only one of her sisters who wasn't bellowing silent obscenities at the Man in White, their restraints stretched to their unbreakable limits. Perhaps they were bellowing at me too. Perhaps they knew about the arrangement I'd made. I looked to my right to see the Man in White standing next to me. He was staring at each of the four girls, in turn, his expression now completely neutral.

The reason Olivia wasn't bellowing, I assume, had something to do with the drip feed that was hooked up to her foot, poking out from under the thin white sheets of her bed. I guessed that was where you attached a drip when a hand wasn't available. The fluttering half-sleep of her eyelids suggested some kind of sedative or painkiller, which would make sense. I'll never know for sure as I didn't ask, and I have—until this very day—done my absolute best to think as little as possible about that awful, terrible hall.

The stumps that were once her arms were heavily bandaged, and her dark hair was tied up on top of her head.

"How did you do it," I asked. My flat voice was barely a croak. "How did you cut them off." My curiosity surprised me, but I had to know nevertheless. I did ask *that.* The Man in White looked at me as if he had forgotten I was there. He looked from me to Olivia and then made the connection.

"Oh, yes," he said, almost absent-mindedly. "A surgeon did it, of course. Fingers are one thing, and they're a good shock technique to begin the Process—shock to the Participant I mean, although of course, it's a big shock to the victim as well—but arms are other things entirely. Depending on the general health of the subject, the shock could potentially kill them if you just cut them away with a saw or whatever. That wouldn't be fair to the Process. No, it's a proper surgical amputation, don't worr—"

The punch couldn't have been that hard. My swing was wild, and my body betrayed me by flinching instinctively as I stepped through with it. However, the blow was unexpected enough that not even Klaus saw it coming. I'm not surprised; I'd been like a kitten for the last two days and had shown zero fire on the way here. *If only they hadn't patted me down* I thought as I fell forward, my foot buckling beneath me. *I could have brought a weapon.* I'd tagged him, at least. As I fell, many hands were already grabbing me, catching me and pulling me away at the same time. I could see that I'd knocked White's sunglasses slightly askew. I couldn't get a look at his face though. He turned immediately away and adjusted his shades, patted his hair, straightened his jacket.

I expected a blow from one of his men as a rebuke, but none came. I'd been pulled about three feet away from the Man in White, and I watched as he straightened up and turned around, his adjustments complete. There was a blooming red spot on his cheek—visible even through the surprised flush of his face overall—and perhaps a tinge of purple blossoming there already. Maybe I'd got him better than I thought. He looked at me... and then turned his gaze to Klaus, who was holding my right arm.

They stared at each other for a moment. Klaus' face didn't change at all under the Man in White's glare.

Then he turned back to me, and the smile crept back onto his face like a spreading puddle of sewage.

"Fair enough," he said, nodding. "I'd like to say *everybody gets one in,* but that wouldn't be true. Even so, that was careless on our part," he said, glancing at Klaus again, "so I think we'll keep you nice and snug like you are right now. At the very least, I think I'll stand over *here,* a-ha ha," he chuckled, pointing at the floor. "Hell, d'you know in all the years we've been carrying out the Process, you're the first one to take *this particular* option, so in my people's defence, this scenario is rather unfamiliar territory. All a bit new to us. Nobody has ever been to a containment centre."

I didn't bother struggling. There were at least six hands on me, and all of them had a grip of iron. I'd hurt him, at least. I hadn't even expected to get that much. My knuckles stung. The Man in White breathed out and clapped his hands together once in a *right then* gesture, and then threw them up in the air.

"O... kay then," he said, his tone one of *well I guess we do* this *next then, yeah? Who knows?* "It was Olivia, you said? Her?" He pointed, and I didn't need to look. I glared at him, then looked at the floor and nodded... and looked straight back up as frenzied movement on my periphery caught my eye. I turned my head to see the other girls in their boxes explode into life, faces red, loose hair sticking to the sweat on their faces that had sprung up as they bellowed and protested in terrified desperation. I guess the soundproofing was somehow only one way. Microphones outside, perhaps. I couldn't even look at them. I thanked God for my balaclava. If they'd seen me, they would have hunted me for the rest of their lives; never mind that those very lives would be entirely owed to me. They wouldn't care about that.

"Do they even know?" I whispered.

"What was that Chris? I'd come closer but, *woah,* y'know."

"Do they even know the situation? Who I am? That someone had to kill to save them?"

"Oh, yeah, yeah they do," the Man in White said, chewing his bottom lip gently as he looked at the girls, thinking about something. "They didn't know you were coming here, or why—we thought that would distress them unduly—but yeah, they know about the Process and that someone's doing it. By the looks of it, though... I think they've figured it out, to be fair. What's happening now, all that."

Silence.

"So..." he said. "You... ready?"

I felt like I was going to faint.

I nodded.

"Okay then," he said, and gestured to the men holding me. I was turned to face Olivia's container.

Her eyes were open and staring right at me.

She was still clearly drugged, but looked as if she were just aware enough. Aware enough to know. Her container began to loom larger and larger as I was brought closer, hobbling towards her. The door looked solid, heavy. Airtight, perhaps.

I started to hyperventilate, but I kept walking.

She's already dead. They're all already dead. That's why she can die. That's why you can do it. This is the Magic Because.

I might as well have been trying to convince myself that I could fly.

We reached the front of the container. Olivia was now actually sitting up in bed, or at least enough as her neck restraint would allow. Her eyes were wider now but blinking, as if the drugs were telling her one thing but her fear was telling her another.

Klaus raised a finger to someone on the opposite side of the hall, and then there was a very faint sound as air was released and the thick door began to swing open. I could hear a steady beeping sound; of course, after major surgery, they'd be careful. She was hooked to a heart monitor. The beeping was fast, drugs or no drugs. Now I could hear the rhythm of her fear.

Don't think. Don't think.

I opened my trembling fingers, and Klaus pushed my paring knife into them; he'd been carrying it all the way from my parents'. That was one of *their* conditions. It had to be my own equipment. He then held the same wrist tightly. There was only one person they were going to allow me to use it on.

"Whu..." I began, then swallowed, closed my eyes, and tried again. "Where should I..."

I looked up at Klaus. He stared back, and then—without taking his eyes off me—he raised his free hand with two of his fingers extended. He then pushed them into the right hand side of his neck. It looked like he was taking his pulse.

I nodded, and they moved me around to the side of the door. They then gently shoved me through, releasing my wrist, and then the door shut quickly behind me. The sound from outside could still be heard, but weakly. There was a small speaker somewhere feeding it through. My microphone theory had been right, even though the only noises coming through were the faint hum of machinery. I heard a slight squeak as the seal re-activated. Olivia was still looking at me. Her heart monitor was beeping faster now.

I moved over and sat down on her side of the bed. My hand was on my lap and so was the knife. Her eyes moved to it, then back to me, blinking slowly. I was so glad she was drugged—I'm still desperately glad to this day—but at the same time, she didn't get to truly be *herself* at the end.

I had to say *something*. Fucking *anything*. And then, of course, there was only one thing to say.

"I'm... I'm so sorry," I whispered. "I can't... I couldn't... and if I didn't, you'd all..." I realized that tears were streaming down my face. I hadn't noticed before. "You see... you're already... you're as good as... It's for the others. If I don't..."

The rhythm of the heart monitor was speeding up even more now. *Beep-beep, beep-beep, beep-beep.* She was aware enough, for sure. She wasn't as gone as I'd hoped. Tears sprung to her eyes too, but she didn't say anything. I gripped the knife, thinking about just lunging in and getting it done, anything to break my paralysis.

Then she clumsily mouthed two words.

"*Do... it.*"

I goggled at her, and then her eyes flicked upwards. Cautiously, stunned, I quickly looked myself. To the right of the air unit in the ceiling, there was a small microphone. One sending sound from the *inside.* It wasn't being broadcast to the hall, but *someone* was listening.

"I don't... wannn..." she said, her words slurred but loud. Loud enough. She shut her eyes and swayed for a moment, then she finished her sentence. "...to die."

I got it. The microphone. She knew the rules. They *had* told her all about the Process.

No suicides. No one who wants to die.

But she did. She did if it would save her sisters. And they couldn't know that.

My arm feeling utterly hollowed, I inched closer to the edge of the bed like an attentive father and raised the knife. I moved it towards her. It shook and shook and shook as if I were going to drop it until the point of it braced against her neck, sitting just above her restraint, steadying my hand. The blade was very sharp, and even in her drugged state, she flinched as the tip pushed gently into her skin. I couldn't look at her, but she was sobbing. The shakes of her body travelled up my noodle-limp arm.

Blood beaded at the tip of the knife.

I was about to kill someone.

Push.

I couldn't.

PUSH.

I did, a little, and Olivia gasped but didn't pull away. The tip of the knife had disappeared about two millimetres, and blood ran from the small incision like a nosebleed.

And again, terribly, I thought I couldn't do it. The Magic Because was useless.

Then Olivia pushed sideways slightly with a cry, enough to have an effect but not enough that anyone watching could truly say if it was me doing the pushing or her, and half of the blade disappeared into her neck with a terrible *give*. The trickle became a gush, and I cried out myself with shock as I found something and pushed now myself, shoving the blade the rest of the way in.

Olivia couldn't make any sound as she twitched gently on the bed. Her eyes rolled over white as crimson fluid practically *sprayed* out from around the knife, silently pumping in a liquid waste of life so violent and horrific to watch that I cannot find the words to describe it. I recoiled, leaping up and off the bed and backing away and *leaving the knife in her neck. I left the fucking knife in there.*

I began to moan, clawing at my face.

Beepbeepbeepbeepbeepbeepbeepbeepbeepbeepbeepbeepbeepbeepbeepbeepbeepbeep

The white pillow and sheets were already covered in red as her armless torso bumped lightly in place, a quiet departure that dropped me to my knees in horror as I began to scream. If not for the sound of the machine, there would have been practically no sound. I remember that very clearly. It made it all so much worse. Then the staccato movement began to slow, becoming bump... bump ... bump. I knew that behind me the other booths out in the hall would now be Pandora's boxes of hate and fury, pain and grief. I closed my eyes and began to rock back and forth, back and forth; the Magic Because a drop of water against the inferno of guilt that would be my world from that day forth.

Beeeeeeeeeeeeeeeeeeeeeeeeeeeeeeeeeeeeeeeeeeeeeeeeeeeeeeeeeeeeeeeeeeee

I balled my hands over my ears, but the sound never went away.

Olivia became still, and the door opened behind me. Hands grasped me firmly, pulling me to my feet and guiding me backwards, but all I saw was that terrible stillness on the bed. Something intangible had left her body, taken by inches of sharp metal. Taken by me.

I started screaming, of course. They closed the door to the container, but I could still see her body through the window. I glanced at the other containers. One look at the screaming, thrashing figures inside was too much. I looked for the Man in White, my eyes bulging sacks of white and red, and found him. He was standing away to my left, closer to the container than me and the men against whom I was straining, his back to us. He was staring through the container window, his arms behind his back.

I wanted to kill him too. I wanted to kill him more than anything in the world.

***

I don't remember much about what happened next.

After a few minutes, I had nothing left. I slumped in their arms. The Man in White said something to me before then, but I couldn't really hear him. I was too hysterical, the edges of my vision becoming grey as I stared at the floor. I could see his feet. All anger, all feeling, was gone. He said something about it being all done, that I'd completed the Process and I wouldn't hear from them again. One thing I did remember though, very clearly:

"Tell no one about this, Chris. That's the final rule. You are - however good your reasons may be - a murderer now. You keep this to yourself, and we will do the same. Keep this to yourself, and all this will never bother you again."

I couldn't speak. He waited for a response, and when there was none, his feet began to walk away from me.

Then he left. Klaus and the others took my stunned and unresisting body home, where I let them remove the body cameras and mic. That was it. That really was it. The Process was over.

The ride back was darkness once more, but this time, it was okay because it was a comfort. Or at least it was until the shock wore off. That came when the sun rose after hours of more blackness in my bedroom. Then I started screaming again, screaming and just *running* around the house.

Have you ever felt helpless against the tortures of your own mind? I mean, really helpless?

Obviously, I didn't go back to work. You know that already. You know what happened for the next few years, in fact. Scotland, all that.

The next five years after the Process were pretty dark, all things considered.

The Man in White and his people were as good as their word. The other girls were released, unharmed, and were found on a country road in Yorkshire by a van driver. There was a big media blitz about it, but I avoided it as much as I could. I was helpless to avoid finding out a few details, though. Overhearing snippets of conversation or being occasionally unable to resist unmuting the news, even though I knew what the aftereffects of it would be on me.

They didn't tell the truth, though. That was always something that got me. The girls, I mean. I'll never know why; were they under threat? Did the Man in White and company have something on them? I don't know. Sure, *I'd* been told that I couldn't tell anyone what had happened, and I'd stuck with it, even years after I was done with The Process. They were very, very clear about that, and I was more than happy to oblige. I had absolutely zero intention of telling anyone anything anyway, and even if I'd felt otherwise, it would have been a small price to pay in order to guarantee never seeing them again. But the girls... I guess I'll never know why they lied.

All I *do* know is that they said Olivia was murdered during their abduction; she'd tried to resist and had been shot in the stomach. She died later in captivity; her body was taken away and the girls made no mention of the Process. Her corpse was never recovered, either. I saw their tearful hugging at the press conference and tried to tell myself that I was the reason they were even able to hug each other. That time, it helped. There were little positive flashes like that, sometimes.

It would have been easier, I think, if I'd killed someone in a rage. A bar fight, perhaps. A traffic accident. But there was something about the *nature* of it, the selection, the action of it, up close and personal. That made all the difference. They'd thought of everything, they really had.

And of course, the questions. The ideas that came in the years that followed.

What about so and so? He was complete scum. Why didn't you do X?

They were endless, but I already told you that. The questions were as pointless as backing away from a fight and saying *why didn't I just go for the eyes.* It's all theory. It's all endless, pointless theory. You have the moment. All you ever have is the moment.

Eventually, the questions became too much, and gave way to a repeated statement that was even worse: *I could have done better, I could have done better, I could have done better.* Then it really *was* too much. I once sat in the bath with a bottle of whiskey and some razor blades, all ready to go. The time I came closest to actually doing it. I couldn't even write a note because I knew I would have to tell everything if I did *and the rules still stood.*

I chickened out. Maybe I would have come close again—maybe I would have even gone through with it eventually—but before I could get that far, I had *the idea*.

Or rather, I absent-mindedly took a flyer from the minimum-wage student giving them out in the street one day, looked at it, and very dimly felt a lightbulb flicker into life in my brain. It went out again fairly quickly; the flyer went straight into my jacket pocket... but more importantly it didn't go in the trash. The seed had been planted, and that flyer was read and reread, as was the accompanying website.

A month later, my application had been approved. I'd had to grin and smile and grimace and bullshit my way through *their* process, but this one was a walk in the park by comparison. It was a breeze after five years of putting on a front whenever I had to deal with people. Three months later, I'd completed their training and preparations. I actually rang my parents and told them about it. They were surprised, to say the least. I didn't blame them. Based on the way I'd lived my life before all this, the underachieving, the attitude, I would have been as surprised as they were.

If I wasn't going to kill myself, but I couldn't get past what I'd done, then I decided that I might as well do something worthwhile with my time. That's too glib; I was desperate. Knowing I couldn't end it all, I had no other choice. I needed something, *anything* that could ease some of my guilt.

And that's how I ended up in Liberia.

It was really, really, difficult. The weather alone was devastating—I've always hated the heat, and that had been a big worry for me before I went there—and as dark a place as I'd been in for a long time, I was still regularly stunned by what I saw. The lives that the kids lived – the ones we worked with - were staggering in their levels of squalor and deprivation. They tried to prepare me before going in, but the reality of being there and seeing it for myself was almost beyond comprehension. It was very nearly too much for me all over again.

I told myself to fucking man up and deal with it, but when I was already at the end of my rope that seemed impossible. It wasn't making things better for me, it was making it worse. The sheer pointlessness of it was staggering. Teaching street kids to read and write, immunizing... what was the point? It was so tiny in the big picture of their lives. They would be crushed by the world no matter what I tried to do. One month in, and after a fourth sleepless night in a row, I decided to terminate my contract.

I wasn't one of the social workers. That required years of training. I was doing the teaching and any of the various bits of dogsbody work that they might send me. The funny thing was that not once in that month had I been asked to drive anyone anywhere, as all of the social workers could either drive themselves or worked with people who did. That was why—on that day of all days, the day I'd decided to quit—getting asked to drive Sheila from the compound because her chaperone had food poisoning always struck me as... well, I don't know. Call it what you will. Coincidence, if you like.

I found myself waiting in the school hallway with a nine-year-old girl named Poady. She wasn't in any of my classes. I'd never seen her before. I had no connection with the kid whatsoever. She was nine, and I'd been asked to sit with her in the school hallway while Sheila met Gardiah—my supervisor—to help her with something. She was swinging her legs as she sat on the bench seating—her feet didn't touch the floor in that seat, she was tiny—her oversized t-shirt covering her like a dress. In fact, she *wore* it like a dress, that t-shirt with a pair of shoes. She was humming to herself. It was stinking hot as usual, and all I was thinking about was how to tell Simon that I was done. The shit would hit the fan, for sure. I'd made a twelve-month commitment, and here I was bailing after one. I wasn't even sure if I was legally allowed, but at the same time, I didn't think they'd keep me here if I didn't want to be.

The door at the other end of the hallway burst open, and a black man and woman came running down the hallway, wide-eyed. Sheila and Gardiah trailed behind, keeping up but remaining at a respectful distance. Poady didn't move, freezing in her seat as the man and woman, presumably a couple, charged towards her. They were crying.

Then the man was upon her, sweeping her up and bellowing, hugging her tightly, and the woman was behind her making a Poady sandwich and now Poady was crying too. I watched the outpouring of joy before me, fascinated. It was like observing some beautiful creature that I thought extinct.

I didn't go through an overnight transformation—things were still very hard for a long time, and I still came close to quitting a few more times after that—but that was the beginning of the change. I finally realized that I wasn't actually here to make things better for *myself*. That had been my excuse for coming, sure, but now I understood that wasn't the fucking point. I finally figured it out. Idiot.

I signed up for another twelve months, and began social worker training at the same time. Things continued to get better.

A new girl, Karen, arrived. She was a teacher as well. I was assigned to show her the ropes. I'd done exactly that and no more. I kept things personable, showing her what she needed to know and having absolutely zero communication outside of that. Hell, I'd stayed away from nearly everyone on the project before then, keeping everything as cordial as possible without ever letting anyone in.

But then one day Karen made an offhand remark as we fell into step beside each other on the way to the cafeteria.

"Hey listen," she said, "thanks for all your help. I know you've got enough to do yourself, but you've really gone above and beyond to help get me settled in."

"Oh, you're welcome," I said, giving one of my standard three-word sentence answers to politely end the interaction. Sometimes, in moments like that, I thought about the old Chris. What would he have said?

"Well, anytime you want dinner, you let me know and it's on me," she said. "Least I can do."

"Ah, I don't really eat," I said, utterly without thinking. I froze as I realized how stupid and rude that sounded. I'd just been in brush-off mode. I wasn't made of stone, even then. She'd been thanking me, after all.

"Oh," she said, and I didn't look at her as we walked. I didn't know what to say. There was a long pause as we walked together. Then she said: "So how the hell are you *alive?*"

I looked at her, speechless, and then I started laughing. It had been so long since I'd done so that it just felt *weird.* She started laughing, too. She was tall for a girl, maybe only an inch or two shorter than me, and her smile when she laughed like that... it was infectious. We went to dinner that night.

I talked more than I had in years. She opened something in me that I'd shut away. Something else I thought The Process had killed.

I signed on for another twelve months. So did she.

We were engaged eleven months later.

I told her everything one month after our engagement.

You wouldn't believe I could, would you? But I did. We were actually in England at the time, in between contracts. Maybe that's a big part of the reason why. My confessing I mean, familiar surroundings triggering memories. Not at home, obviously—I didn't want to tell them that I was back—but in her home city of Derby. She wanted to introduce me to her parents. I'd told her that mine were away on a cruise, and what a shame, and lousy timing.

It wasn't home, but even driving through the Midlands was enough to put me on edge. Road signs to Coventry near Birmingham airport – we couldn't get flights to East Midlands - the mild to medium accent; all of it meant that I wasn't myself at all. It reminded me of why I'd left in the first place. When I was away, the pain in England could be thought of as a dream.

We made it to her parents' in the suburb of Robinson, a mildly famous pace ever since that crazy guy's diary got published several years earlier. I'd smiled and 'yes, indeed'-ed my way through dinner with her Mum and Dad—I'd had enough practice with my own folks to be good at it when I had to be—and Karen seemed pleased... but she only laughed when her parents laughed, only asked questions when her parents did. It wasn't until later, as I slid in beside her under the twenty-year-old duvet in the house's spare room, that she finally spoke up. I hadn't said a word to her since dinner. I couldn't. I felt like I was vibrating with tension. The effort of feeling normal was killing me.

"You don't like them, do you?" she asked with a sigh. She wasn't angry, I could tell; more as if she thought her parents had failed in their duty to impress. "Look, I know they're a bit stiff, and Mum can be hard work until she's had a drink, but it's only because she doesn't know—"

"They're fine, they're great," I said, as kindly as I could. I was torn between feeling bad – I'd actually thought her parents were really nice – and panic. What should I say? "I'm just not feeling very well." That was the best I could do, and it was as transparent as it could possibly be. Karen propped herself up on one elbow, lit by the half-light from outside. Her straight brown hair falling over her face.

"It's okay, but don't bullshit me," she said, a slight edge in her voice now. "What was it they said? I won't be offended or anything, just be honest."

My mind went blank, and to my total and utter surprise, I felt my chest begin to constrict so hard that it hurt. My breathing sped up, and I began to feel a sensation of total panic as years of nothing but oppressed thoughts and feelings suddenly added up and my body said *fuck it.*

"Chris? Chris, what the hell? Calm down, it's ok, it's ok!" She turned on the lamp, which I didn't like. I winced, and continued struggling to breathe. "Ok, try and tell me, do I need to call an ambulance?" she said urgently, leaning over me. "Can you tell me? Do you know what's happening? Wait, that's two questions, shit, do you need an ambulance?" I was already trying to calm my breathing, knowing that this had to be a panic attack, so I shook my head no... but it went on for a while, Karen trying to soothe, me trying to stop her from calling anyone. Once I'd calmed down, she was silent, her head on my chest. I knew she wanted to ask questions but didn't want to risk setting me off again.

I'd known when I'd asked her to marry me that I'd probably tell her one day, rules or no rules. I just wanted to marry her first. I could trust *her* to keep it secret. I wanted us to be together always.

But tonight had shown me that I could only keep it a secret for so long.

"I have something I need to tell you," I said quietly. "It's going to sound utterly insane, and I don't know what you're going to think of me afterwards. If you believe me, you might think I did the right thing, as awful as it was. As... as much as it ruined my life. If you don't believe me, you're going to think I'm crazy and you will never want to see me again."

"I know you're not crazy," she said, her voice resonating in my chest as she stroked at my arm with her fingers. There was silence. I took a deep breath, her head rising as I did so. Her pretty head. Her beautiful face.

"When I was younger, a man dressed in a white came to my parents' house."

I talked her through the whole thing, from start to finish. She didn't say a word, apart from freezing against me and drawing in near-silent but sharp intakes of breath at some of the more shocking points. By the time I got to the end, tears were streaming down my face. She still hadn't spoken.

But her fingers were still stroking my arm.

"I'm glad you told me," she said.

"Do you believe me?" I asked.

"Chris," she said, and sat up. She shifted forward on the bed, and took my face in her hands. "I've heard horror stories ever since I landed in Liberia. Ever since I joined the organization. Lunatics, people who have inflicted unbelievable cruelties on women and children just because they can. I've seen the results. I've seen the victims." She leaned down and kissed my forehead, then moved back slightly and looked into my eyes. "A lot of people wouldn't believe what you've told me because they can't believe anyone could be so pointlessly and deliberately... well, evil. I know better." She leaned down and wrapped her arms around me, and I felt something move through my entire body and leave. A ghost of something; not all of it, but a lot. I felt lighter. I hadn't been cleansed, but my soul had been given a light once-over. "I believe you," she said in my ear, and I felt wetness against my cheek. I wrapped my arms around her.

I'll never forget that night. Ever. My Karen. *Karen.*

A year later, we were married. It was—obviously—a very small ceremony in France. I think Karen was sad about that. She hid it but I knew she would have preferred a big wedding back home. Instead, there were only a few guests; her parents, a few friends, our work colleagues... and *my* parents. Things changed some between them and myself after I'd told Karen about the Process. I'd *never* tell *them* the truth, but the ice I'd built to keep my parents at bay had melted once I'd unburdened myself to my other half. I will never forget seeing their faces after Karen and I were pronounced husband and wife, my Dad grabbing me on the way back down the aisle and just laughing and laughing. I grabbed his arm back, laughing myself, amazed that I could not only be happy again, but *this* happy. At night everyone danced. The honeymoon was bliss, apart from an argument with the hotel staff about a room upgrade we'd been promised not being available. I didn't care, but Karen had a tendency to go ballistic about that kind of thing.

To everyone's surprise, we went back to Liberia. I wasn't done, and Karen was happy to come with me. In the back of my mind, I wondered about what would happen the day she decided she'd had enough, that she wanted to start a family back home. I wondered how she would react when I told her I didn't think I'd ever be done. Part of me would wonder, however, if that would always be true; if it wouldn't fade with time. Then I'd get confused, push it all away, and carry on with whatever I'd been doing. That went on for two years; us in our little shared unit in the compound, friends around us that I was – finally - starting to let in. Life was pretty much wonderful. There were downsides: I got caught in a riot and thought I was going to be crushed to death when I fell down in the middle of it, and one time Karen used my story of the Process against me in an argument. I won't repeat what she said, but that was so devastating—even though her face was shock and horror when she realized what she'd done—that I nearly walked out the door and never came back. We got through it, got past it, and were very much in love.

We were happy.

Then seven days ago, during a lunch break in my empty classroom as I was marking some papers, the Man in White came to see me.

***

Chapter Seven: The Exit Interview

***

I don't know how he managed it; the security we have at the school is excellent. Cameras, personnel; the former strangely offline and the latter strangely engaged elsewhere, all at the wrong moment. But in he came. Klaus, of course, was with him.

I heard the door open, and I looked up.

At first, it just didn't make any sense. There were no thoughts to go along with the image before me. I had the same feeling about it that you would get looking at an old poster for a movie that you knew. Then I saw the slight movement of their shoulders as they breathed, and the shift in their weight as they came to a stop just inside the doorway. The skin moving around a spreading smile that I recognised all too well.

Even as I struggled for breath, as I went to push myself away from my desk on instinct and flatten myself against the wall, as I only succeeded in knocking my pencil holder to the floor with a spreading clatter of rolling graphite and wood... I noticed all the things that had changed. They were pretty much impossible to miss. The wheelchair, for a start.

Klaus was pushing the Man in White before him; the large man's oak-like frame slightly stooped in order to reach the handles. The thought flashed across my mind, even through my panic: *all your resources and you don't have an electric wheelchair?*

They aren't paying you enough swiftly followed by *why, why, oh God why can't you leave me alone, I did everything you asked me to so why can't you leave me alone.*

And horribly, I realized that last part wasn't true. It wasn't true at all.

The Man in White's need for his current transport was immediately obvious. I'd never been sure if he'd worn a wig, but either the wig had been removed to reveal his true physical nature, or the thick hair had fallen out due to his current condition. Either way, the majority of it was now gone, and all that was left were a few thin wisps. I didn't need him to tell me. It was obvious. The pallor of his skin, the cheekbones that stuck out like knuckles on either side of that horrible grin which somehow remained intact while the rest of him fell apart, all of it said only one thing: the Man in White was dying.

Instead of making me feel better, that thought made me worse. He was crazy before, but a man with nothing left to lose is a man on the edge. I knew this from personal experience. Klaus, of course, hadn't changed a bit. I felt like this would still be the case if I shot him in the face at point-blank range.

I continued on my wild backwards trajectory, falling back to let the wall take my weight, but I miscalculated. It was further away than I thought, and I clattered to the ground like my pencils. I landed hard, and was dimly aware of the sound of the classroom door closing. I didn't want to get back up, as that would mean seeing them again and having to deal with the nightmare that had followed me all the way to Liberia, but I was already springing to my feet and moving around to the far end of my desk. I still couldn't breathe, despite whooping in huge lungfuls of air that didn't actually seem to carry any oxygen. My chest was tight, and I realized that—ridiculously—I'd snatched up one of my pencils and was now holding it tightly in my fist, holding it before me in a trembling hand as if to fend them off. The pair of them didn't move and nobody had spoken yet. We stood like this for a few moments; the only sound was my gasping panic.

"Hello, Chris," the Man in White said, and although that used-car salesman tone was still there, his voice was weaker. Thinner. "You'll have to pardon the indulgence here, but... surprise." He held up both gloved hands, lifting them upright at the wrists without moving his forearms. He was dressed exactly the same as before, as was Klaus. I almost thought that – judging by the rest of him – that the suit should be worn out too, perhaps turned to a brownish off-white that had slowly stained irretrievably into the fabric over the years. But of course, it was pristine. The money he saved on wheelchairs obviously went into keeping his wardrobe stocked up.

"Muh," I said, leaning forward and putting one hand on the desk to steady myself. "Muh. *Muh.*" The room actually began to spin. I closed my eyes, partly to try to get a grip and partly to try and pointlessly will the moment into oblivion.

It's trauma. They aren't here. This is just a freakout. It's all finally catching up with you. It's probably a good thing. There's no reason for them to be here. You followed all the rul—

But you didn't, did you?

I opened my eyes. They were still standing there, and seemed even more present now that Klaus had let go of the wheelchair and straightened up to his full height. I noticed a fine sheen of sweat on Klaus' forehead, and realized that they must have been dying outside in the heat wearing those jackets. They obviously hadn't been inside long; the school's air conditioning must have been heavenly to them.

"Take a moment, if you need it," the Man in White said, each word clearly requiring a little more effort than the one before. "Apologies for startling you. Obviously, we couldn't exactly phone ahead. However, we won't be disturbed for a while. We aren't going to do anything right now Chris, we just want a little chat. So please, relax." He looked up at Klaus for a moment, and gestured to one of the school desks. Klaus nodded, and walked over to rest his enormous bulk on the desk's surface. It creaked a little. I turned as he did so, holding the pencil out towards him, its tip wavering spastically in the air. Klaus looked at it for a moment, then to my astonishment—in a gesture so small that I nearly missed it—briefly raised a hand and nodded at me in greeting. I was so surprised that I was immediately disarmed. I slowly lowered the pencil to my side and placed it on top of the desk.

They know that you—

I tried to reassure myself. They'd told me that - for that moment at least - they just wanted to talk. And from the little I knew about the Man in White and whoever his employer was, they were at least as good as their word. Fucking insane, but as good as their word.

"That's good, Chris," I heard the Man in White say, and I turned to look at his dying face, hidden behind his bug glasses as always. "Put the weapon down," he added with a chuckle, and a rage bloomed inside me that I could barely contain. Were it not for Klaus, in that moment, I don't know what I would have done. But then, that's kind of been the point all along, hasn't it?

"Get... out... of... my classroom..." I managed, needing both arms now to hold myself up, my fingers clawing into the wood and my voice cracking.

"We will Chris, we will," White said, his hands flapping up again, hinging at the wrists like the foils on a passenger plane. "I promise. I'll say what I have to say, and then what comes later will come later. Okay? I just have a few things to ask you, and then we will have a few things to *discuss*. And then we'll leave, one way or the other. Okay?"

I didn't know what to say, rage or not. I looked at Klaus, who was as inscrutable as ever. I was still trembling, but now it was with anger.

"What the fuck is this?" I hissed. "I *did* your stupid fucking task. I killed—" I caught myself and dropped my voice to a whisper. "I *killed her,* I *killed her,* and the deal is all done, so *why are you here you sick fuck? Leave me alone!"* My hands were off the desk now, balled into fists. My nails were cutting into my skin.

"I understand your concerns Chris, I genuinely do," White said, and he'd done the old switcheroo once more; gone was the salesman, here was the father figure. Were I not so angry, I would have been thoroughly impressed. "You must be wondering what the hell is going on, and of course I'm going to tell you. Let me assure you though, we are absolutely not, in any way, going back on our part of the bargain." The smile crept back now, but only slightly. "On *our* part of the bargain." He repeated, quietly. I felt the insect eyes boring into mine, and my anger disappeared like piss in the rain. Rage drained out through my feet, pushed by the terror that filled my veins in an instant.

He knows he knows he fucking knows he fucking knows

You don't know that! He doesn't know anything! How could he?

But I also knew just how resourceful the Man in White could be. I didn't say anything, hoping my face revealed nothing, but I knew that wasn't the case. The son of a bitch even nodded. He knew. I opened my mouth to say *wait,* to explain, but the Man in White was one step ahead as always.

"You're a married man now, aren't you Chris?"

Shit. Shit. Oh God, oh shit

"...that ...that's none of your business." It was supposed to sound brave, it was supposed to sound forceful, but all I heard was guilt. I'd broken the rules, and everyone in the room knew it.

"Well, the fact of your marriage isn't, certainly," the Man in White said, cocking his head slightly so that some of the wisps of hair on his thin skin fell sideways, "that's nothing to do with us. Congratulations, by the way. That was unexpected, certainly. But yes, that's none of our business. It's only *our business...* that is, you know. Our business."

"Wait... wait..." I stammered, holding up a hand, but he just kept talking, all the Man ever did was *keep talking,* could he not just stop for once and leave me alone?

"A good marriage... what do they all say is the key to a good marriage, eh? Hell, what do they all say is the key to a good *relationship,* let alone a marriage? Heh, not that we'd really know, right?" He addressed this last part to Klaus, who turned to face White and moved his head in a silent chuckle. The Man in White snapped his fingers gently, then wagged one at Klaus. "Hold on a second, I just thought, goodness me. What was it he called you?" White looked back at me. "What did you call him? I can't remember. Heinrich? Something like that?" I just gaped at him, not wanting this diversion to end, anything to halt the Man in White's previous speech, but then he had it. "*Klaus!*" he cried, laughing openly. "Klaus, that was it! Fantastic, fantastic." Klaus smiled a little, then turned back to face me. By the time we locked eyes to sunglasses once more, Klaus' smile was gone.

"Ah, dear," said the Man in White wistfully, shaking his head with a smile. "Anyway, where was I? *Marriage,* yes, yes." He shifted in his wheelchair slightly, then refocused his gaze on me. "*Communication,*" he said, and I knew for certain that I was utterly doomed. "Communication is key, isn't it Chris? A couple that talks, works. Am I right?"

I had no words, only a dry mouth and an overpowering sense of time running out.

Karen, oh my God, I tried to protect you but I couldn't hold it in anymore and now it's all coming home to roost.

"You remember what we told you at the end of the Process, don't you Chris? We were very clear about that. You have to remember. I know you remember. Right?"

I opened my mouth to protest, trying wildly to think of excuses, a loophole, but none came. After a few moments of silence, the Man in White spoke again.

"I'll take that as a yes," he said, nodding. The smile was completely gone, the blank mask pulled out of his bag of facial tricks and worn with style. "And you *have* to be wondering how I could know, yes? You have to be wondering how I know you told your wife all about everything you did. Or, perhaps you're wondering *if* I know you told your wife all about everything you did. About *us.*"

I glanced at Klaus, who had stood up.

They promised they wouldn't do anything. They promised that this was just a talk.

Then the next thought:

They promised that this was just a talk right now.

"Wait..." I said again, my voice breaking loudly now. "*Please.*"

"Before we go any further, Chris," the Man in White said with a sigh, looking at the cuffs of his jacket and adjusting them pointlessly, "I'm going to ask you a question. Okay? And I want you to answer it honestly. We may already know the answer, we may not. You don't *have* to answer, of course, but that is in itself a form of deceit in our book, and so it will be taken as lying. Okay? Do you understand? Are you ready for the question?"

"You... you have no right to do this," I whispered from nowhere, but it was pointless. I realized they had me because of Karen. It was all because of her, and because of fear *for* her. I knew again—right there in that moment and with absolutely crystal clarity and diamond-hard certainty—that I could kill the Man in White.

"Did you tell your wife what you did, Chris?" the Man in White asked. The question was flat and devoid of all inflection. I wondered crazily if the man was a robot, one at the end of its lifecycle, its broken and denaturing circuits showing themselves in the slow decay of the pretend flesh on top.

My mouth worked silently.

He can't know. He can't know.

If you tell him the truth, he'll definitely know.

If you lie, it could be worse.

What. The fuck. Do I—

"Yes," I heard myself say, my eyes shut tight. "Yes, I told her. I couldn't help it. I had to. I was dying inside. I tried not to. It just came out. You asked too much of me in the first place, and keeping it a secret was even more than that. I didn't expect to get..." My eyes opened, and when I spoke again my only thought was of a desperate, desperate love for my wife. "Please. *Please.* Don't hurt her."

"You knew the rules, Chris. We have been as good as our word."

"You did all this! Fuck you!" I screamed. *"You ruined everything, you ruined my life! Fuck you! Fuck you!"* I beat at the table with my fists. I snatched up a stapler and threw it at the Man in White, but Klaus moved faster than I could see and caught it. I didn't even flinch, and carried on screaming. Klaus slowly sat back down, holding the stapler as if he didn't even know it was there. *"Don't you touch her! Don't you touch my fucking wife!"*

The Man in White cocked his head to one side, drew in a deep breath, let it out. He stared at me as I stood there breathing heavily. In a distant, rational part of my mind, I decided that I could maybe – *maybe* – if I went around the side of the desk that was away from Klaus, if I was *really* fast, then I could drive a pencil into White's throat. It was the slimmest of chances, but I was going to try. I was going to let them think I was beaten, and then I would at least—

"*Have* we ruined your life, Chris?"

"...what?"

"You said we'd ruined your life. How did we ruin it?" The Man in White's arms left the rests of the wheelchair for a moment, and folded in front of a chest that no longer filled its shirt the way it once did. I was so confused that I became annoyed. I had enough, e-fucking-*nough.*

"Jesus, *what?*" I cried, exasperated beyond endurance. "What is this now? Can't you just... *please...*"

"What did you have before, Chris?" White asked, shrugging. "A shitty job with a shitty boss? The same shitty friends that you grew up with, ones that you never had anything in common with in the first place? Where was your ambition? What were your goals? Hell, forget goals and ambition, where was your *passion?*" An expression I'd never seen before—not even when I'd managed to punch him in the face in that awful building of torture and death many years ago—began to spread across the Man in White's face. A scowl. Genuine contempt. "What actually mattered to you? What made you *alive*? What made you any more than a total waste of potential and flesh?"

"*That's* none of your fucking business either!" I blurted, and I remember clearly thinking *screw it* as I began to walk around the table towards White. Klaus stood up and held out a hand, but I gave him the finger. "Fuck y—" I began.

"We're not going to touch her, Chris," I heard the Man in White say, hidden behind Klaus' towering frame. "We're not going to touch her, and we're not going to touch you." My finger lowered, more confused than ever. "It doesn't really matter if you told your wife anyway. I just wanted you to come clean. Hell, Chris, we *expected* you to tell her. It was all in your profile." I looked up into Klaus' face, as unreadable as an Easter Island statue. He watched me as he moved aside, revealing a now-smiling dying man.

"You... you gave..." I gasped, wanting to say *you gave me a chance to come clean, who the fuck do you think you are* but not getting it. I just wanted answers. What the hell was going on? "The... test? The test you made me do at the start of..." I couldn't say *the Process*. I wouldn't.

"You *must* know that you weren't picked at random, Chris," the Man in White said, screwing up his forehead in mild derision. "Surely? I mean, we told you that you were picked because you were ordinary, but you can't possibly think that was the only reason." He shook his head. "No, no. Do you think that we would just pick someone *ordinary enough* out of nowhere and put them through the Process? All off the back of one solitary test that you did at your kitchen table, no matter how insightful and in-depth? We'd watched you for a *year* before we came to you, Chris." He raised his eyebrows at me, enjoying my obvious surprise. "All your emails. All your phone calls. All your bullshit social interactions that amounted to nothing. All your 'friends' with whom you had no actual connection whatsoever." He held his hands up. "I don't mean to be disrespectful Chris, and I'm not saying this to get under your skin. I'm saying it because it's true. And I think you know this already. You've thought about your old life over the years since the Process, haven't you? Since you came here? You must have."

I wanted to say he was wrong. I wanted to say he knew nothing. But not only was he right about my old life—I knew this in the very core of my bones—but he was right about the fact that I'd looked back since the Process. I'd seen a man I didn't remember, and people that seemed as empty as ghosts, but I'd blamed those thoughts on the Process itself. I only felt that way because of the trauma, I'd always told myself. They had stolen it all from me. It had all been a terrible loss. But as soon as I'd heard the word *connection,* it had stuck me like the knife I'd jammed into the neck of Olivia MacArthur. Where had my connections been with those past friends, other than the weight of history? Nowhere.

But so fucking what? Therefore, I deserved to be forced to murder someone?

"What... what are you talking about?" I whispered. "What does that have to do with anything?" I threw up my arms, tears coming to my eyes as I reached the breaking point. "Why are you *here,* why are you here..." It was a moan.

"I'm dying, Chris," the Man in White said, the grin completely insane against the seriousness of his words. "I think I don't need to tell you that, am I right?" He actually chuckled at this, his tone that of a man asking *hot enough for ya?* "Of course I don't. And there *is* no employer. There is no one pulling the strings. You're talking to the man at the top. The Process is my creation and my creation alone."

In a daze, I looked at Klaus for confirmation of this. He nodded slowly and sagely in return. I found myself nodding back mindlessly, returning the action like a simpleton.

"Participants used to ask so many questions when they knew it was *my* idea," White said, sighing as he did so and sounding like someone saying *the commute is just such a pain in the ass.* "I realized that a much easier way to get *on* with things was to say hey, don't blame me, I'm just the messenger, this is the situation and here we go. Same with our outfits. If you look like a movie villain, people accept a crazy situation more easily if it's something they recognize. Plus, it's intimidating, the sunglasses hide your face, yadda yadda yadda. Lots of advantages," he said, waving his hand and dismissing his own point. "Also, you know. Stylish."

"You don't think you're a villain? You really don't think you're a villain?" I coughed.

"Oh, I'm a monster. No doubt about it," the Man in White scoffed, shrugging. "I'm also a man of considerable means, Chris. This you probably also know. I mean it's obvious. You've seen enough of my network to know that, and you've seen hardly *any* of it. I've lasted much, much longer than the doctors gave me, certainly, years and years, but I've been carrying out this work ever since the diagnosis. And you, and all the people before you, and the ones after you – for of course there were many more after you, many more – were all a part of what I consider to be my life's work." My legs gently bumped up against a desk as I listened, my mind hypnotized by the Man in White's words. I'd never given up on them coming for me, never *really* given up, and now here they were; not with violence and demands, but *answers.* I was rapt.

"We have people in Universities looking out for us, Chris. People in places of work," White continued. "They give us names of people who they think fit the bill, and we watch. And we drill it down, and drill it down, and drill it down, until we have our Candidates. Then *we* watch, and take in all the information that we can, the same way that we did with you. That test on day one, the one you took in your kitchen… that's the final, final check to see if someone has the right profile to be an actual Participant. You probably won't like this, but if you hadn't scored the way you did that morning, none of this would have happened. We would have walked right out of the door. We would have ended your

Process and someone else would have tried to save the girls. We always have alternates. Always."

My legs nearly gave way, and I think I would have fallen again if not for the desk holding me up.

"I was like you, Chris. *I was like you,*" White continued. "And I have to say, that isn't exactly a compliment. Actually, I was worse, because I was wealthy too. Rich and selfish. Two of the prime characteristics that make up the worst examples of humanity. Coasting along, coasting along." He raised his eyebrows as if to say *sound familiar?* I didn't respond, so he shrugged and continued.

"Once I got my diagnosis, I met people, Chris. Obviously, I had the best doctors in the world, but ...along the way I met the people who *didn't* have the money for that kind of thing, didn't have the money to buy help. The people who relied on the people that *gave.* The people who relied on the volunteers." He lifted his head slightly and looked at the ceiling, and for the first time ever I thought he sounded truly sincere. "The volunteers... the ones that make a *difference.* And all because of nothing but their own kindness."

He sighed, and appeared to forget that anybody else was there for a moment. When he eventually looked back at me, his brow was furrowed behind his sunglasses. "And therein lay the problem Chris," the Man in White said, his voice weary for once. "It drove me insane thinking about it. I mean I'd lie awake night after night... anyway, anyway. The point is this: *yes,* there are people out there that will always volunteer, people who were born with the good of their fellow man on their minds. *But there are never enough and there never will be.* Do you understand? You can pay people to do it — and I do — but that's not the same. You'll never get that level of care, that level of personal commitment, the level of desire that truly makes the difference. And even pay won't attract enough people to dirty jobs in dangerous areas. Unless someone is born to be one of those naturally gifted carers, they will never become one. There will only ever be *so many...* unless someone creates them." He stared at me, and as the smile slowly crept back onto his face, a funny thing happened. Even now, I feel disgusted at the thought of it, but this is how it happened. Nothing more.

Despite my confusion, despite my anger, I felt a kind of... *lifting* sensation. As his words resonated with me, something began to move inside me, something that just didn't make any true sense yet *absolutely did,* a Magic Because that was absolutely and totally insane and yet it was something, *something...*

There was a reason for all of this, a reason, a reason, a reason...

ARE YOU FUCKING KIDDING ME? HAVE YOU SUDDENLY FORGOTTEN WHAT THEY DID?

It was madness. These men were monsters. I thought of the work I'd done and the lives I'd touched already and the man I'd become *and there was still so much more to do, so much more I wanted to do,* and I didn't know what to say.

"Why are you here?" I whispered, the confusion inside too much to deal with.

"We don't call it the Process because we get people to commit murder, Chris," the Man in White said, and the smile that had seemed so punchable, so hateful, suddenly seemed as if it had been partially filtered. It didn't have quite the same poisonous effect. My hands left the desk and clenched into fists, unclenched, clenched. "We call it the Process because it's ongoing. And it doesn't end with someone dying. That's when the Process *begins*. That's when the mental transmogrification starts, and a higher reasoning and understanding is achieved. And that's when the *work* begins."

"You're insane," I whispered, but it was barely audible. The Man in White chuckled quietly in response.

"I can't deny that there's a very strong possibility you're right there," he said, cocking his corpse's skull to one side in a whimsical manner. "It's not exactly the most regular recruitment plan in the world, I grant you. And hey, there are probably many other ways of doing it. But this is the way that I feel is best, and that is the way I have executed my will. And you know all about that line of thinking, don't you?" He nodded as if I'd agreed with him. "Anyway, the results speak for themselves. I've had to start more projects like this," he said, gesturing around himself to the classroom that currently housed the three of us, "than you might think. It's the knock-on effect, Chris. Each one of you usually creates another, you know. Wait, I don't mean..." He formed two bony fingers into a gun and mimed a gunshot. "Not *that*. No, I mean you tend to *inspire*. Have you done that yet?" I hadn't. I felt ashamed... then remembered again that I should feel angry and tried to cling to that. It was more difficult now though, slippery to the touch. As if reading my mind, the Man in White waved his own words away. "Not yet. You haven't yet. Of course not. But you will."

"You started this centre?" I asked, feeling like a rat in a maze.

"It wasn't *coincidence* that you heard about the organization, Chris," White said. "We always make sure of that. There are ways to push you towards us. Of course, you can volunteer elsewhere, and that's still great, but we prefer you, our Participants, to end up with us."

"You ruined my life..." I muttered again, but it was weak, for the Man in White's words were already repeating themselves in my head:

Have we ruined your life, Chris?

And the answer came back to me like a tolling bell:

Karen.

The woman that was my world, delivered by the Process.

I became very still and strangely calm.

"I don't think we did, Chris," the Man in White said. "We put you in an extremely difficult position, and you ended up doing a terrible thing for what you believed were the right reasons. And they *were* the right reasons, you know that. And let me be clear: while we are aware that your life is far better now in all the ways that matter, I am not here expecting you to thank us. You *should* hate us. You *should* want revenge. Which *is* the reason we're here." The Man in White nodded at Klaus, who stood and reached into his pocket. I didn't flinch. When Klaus' gloved hand emerged again, it was holding a sheathed knife. He held it out to me handle first. With a shaking hand, I took it.

"I'm doing the rounds, Chris," the Man in White said, his thin voice sounding as cheery and crazy as he clearly was. "Tying up loose ends, as it were. Sorry, that sounds bad too. I'm really making a hash of my words today. I mean... well, firstly going around to all of the Participants and telling them the truth. The ones that are still alive anyway. We did have two suicides that their profiles really didn't predict. I only have a year or two left now at best – even I have to accept that – and so I just really wanted to have the satisfaction of letting them know the purpose of all this. Call me sentimental, call me arrogant, and to be honest it's probably a little from column A and a little from Column B. I won't tell the most recent two or three Participants yet, they need a few years to get further along the Process, but someone will if I'm gone before then. Oh, the *organization* will keep going—as will the Process project—it just won't be run by me. Ah, sorry," he waved his hand dismissively and then pinched the bridge of his nose with his fingers, a rare but brief show of weakness. "I got sidetracked didn't I? I was explaining the two reasons why I'm going around to everyone and got stuck on the first. No, the *second* reason is... well... that." He pointed at the knife in my hand. I looked down at it as if it were a freshly laid turd that I'd just discovered I was holding for some reason.

"Fair is fair," he said, and the smile was gone again. "You can do it right now. No one will come in, and we will clean everything up. *Klaus* won't lift a finger to stop you. He is under strict instruction not to intervene."

I looked from White to Klaus, White to Klaus, dumbfounded. A few minutes ago, I thought they were here to kill me. Now it was clear that the case was very much the opposite of that.

"You... you want me to end it for you?" I whispered.

"No, no, goodness no," White scoffed. "I have plenty of people to do that. Heck, I could do it myself. No, I have a few years left, and given the choice, personally I'd like to see them out, thank you very much. But as I said: *fair is fair.* We forced ourselves into your life, Chris. We made a decision to place you in that scenario and you paid the price. You have, however—dare I say—reaped the rewards, but that isn't the point. I am proud of my life's work, profoundly and passionately, but I know that I have never, ever had the right to do any of the terrible things that I have done, no matter what the goal or purpose. And so I have to, at the very least, offer myself to be subjected to the same... treatment that your victim experienced."

"My *what?*"

"Sorry, Olivia. Poetic justice, either way. Like I said. Sentimental, perhaps."

I pulled the knife from its sheath. To my total lack of surprise, it was a paring knife, identical to the one I'd used to murder Olivia MacArthur. I didn't even know they *made* sheaths for paring knives.

"I believe in fairness, and I believe in finishing a job," White said, as if from very far away. I was captivated by the blade as it reflected the cheap lighting in the ceiling, much the same as it had reflected the strip lighting in that terrible hall or barn or whatever the hell it was. "My own Process is nearly complete, Chris. Visiting you all – giving you all a *real* choice, for once – is a part of that. Fair is fair."

I looked at him. I looked at Klaus, who nodded again. I felt the weight of the knife in my hand, the reality of it.

"There's nothing *fair* here, even if I kill you, so stop fucking saying 'fair is fair,'" I said, my voice, flat and lifeless. "Wait... why aren't you dead already? Why didn't one of the others kill you? The ones you told before me?"

"Well, one of them was dead, as I say - the other suicide was after you – and the rest, what was it, Klaus?" White asked, as if discussing the sign-up sheet for the office fantasy football league. "Eleven or so we've seen so far? About half of them couldn't stomach the idea of killing again, even if it was me, and the other half kind of wanted to but, y'know..." His hands went up and took in the classroom again. "They're not *grateful* and I don't blame them at all, but... they can't deny the change that was made. They're in places like this. Fulfilled in ways they never had been before. Their lives have meaning. They've had a lot longer to go through the Process, like I said."

"And if I kill you, the next guy...?" These questions were crazy, but logic wanted to know, my brain operating the same way it had on those dark few days ten years ago. White shrugged.

"Well geez Chris, I can only be killed so many times, gimme a break," he chuckled. "Someone will go and explain to them what this has all been about, and pass on the good news that I've been killed by someone else." I suddenly felt jealous of whoever heard that. Whoever had already had the choice removed but still got the *good news*.

The room was silent.

Wait, this is a choice? You actually have to think about this? Are you kidding me? Are you fucking kidding me? YOU KNOW YOU CAN KILL HIM, HE DESERVES TO DIE, HE'S RUINED COUNTLESS LIVES—

And I would have another death on my conscience. But the Process project would continue anyway.

I found myself suddenly wondering about other missing people cases. Other people I'd heard of in the news over the years, murdered without motive or just plain vanished. How many of them were to do with this man? How many were victims, how many were Participants who had run away like I had?

I thought about Olivia MacArthur, the way her limbless and helpless torso twitched on the bed to which she was shackled, spraying blood from a knife wound in her neck.

I thought about my life, my wife, my work.

My hand tightened around the knife's grip.

And then the blade trembled.

"Okay, it looks like you need some time to think. That's not a problem. We'll come back in a week, Chris," White said. "Telling the police here will be pointless. Try it and see. Anyway; think about it. The choice is yours."

They left.

That was six days ago.

***

It's now 5:30 am as I write, and my wife lies asleep in bed a few feet away from me. I am sitting in a small, battered armchair in the corner of our tiny room at the compound, the air conditioning creaking and bellowing as always, hanging on for dear life. Karen lies under thin but handmade blankets that were given to us as gifts by a grateful parent; they were hugely appreciated as a replacement for the military grade sheets we were given when we moved in. Our home is one room with a bathroom whose plumbing is the neediest I have ever encountered.

It is my home. It is my life, and I love it.

I haven't told Karen that the Man in White came back. I haven't told her because I don't know what I am going to do. The sheathed knife is in my pocket. I keep finding it in there.

Tomorrow, they will come to see me for the last time. One way or another.

I think about the pair of them forcing their way into my life. I think about the staggering arrogance of deciding - whatever the motive - that someone's life is yours to manipulate. I think about the evil of what was done to those girls. I think of Olivia MacArthur's face. I think of the endless nights.

I think of these things, and I see my hand around the knife's handle, my knuckles white as I jam the blade into the Man in White's face, twisting and dragging it sideways as I make it as painful as possible in an attempt to force that smile away.

Then my wife sighs in her sleep, or rolls over, and I am brought back here. I think of the lives I have touched. I think of purpose. I think of happiness, not the return of it, but the *arrival* of it, for I was never truly happy – not even close – before.

They took everything. They gave me everything.

My fists clench, unclench, clench, unclench.

I am not a killer, yet I am.

I think I know what my choice is.

In the morning, when the Man in White comes to me again, he will have his answer.

Right now I am going to get into bed beside my wife and hold her close. I will whisper to her that I love her.

And then I will sleep deeply and well.

*

IF YOU ENJOYED THIS BOOK, PLEASE LEAVE A STAR RATING ON AMAZON; LUKE SMITHERD IS STILL SELF-PUBLISHED AND COULD USE ALL THE HELP HE CAN GET... SO IF YOU FEEL LIKE HELPING OUT (THANK YOU!) YOU CAN DO SO ON THE BOOK'S AMAZON PAGES! AND SOME GOOD NEWS; IF YOU DID ENJOY THIS BOOK, YOU MIGHT LIKE TO TRY ONE OF LUKE SMITHERD'S OTHER

NOVELS, **THE STONE MAN**. *READ ON PAST THE AUTHOR'S AFTERWORD FOR THE BEGINNING CHAPTER OF THAT VERY BOOK!*

AND HEY! MORE FREE STUFF! WANT TO GET A ***FREE STORY*** FROM LUKE SMITHERD, AND ALSO FIND OUT ABOUT HIS OTHER AVAILABLE BOOKS AS AND WHEN THEY'RE RELEASED (AND OFTEN GET *THOSE* FOR FREE AS WELL?)? THEN VISIT LUKESMITHERD.COM AND SIGN UP FOR THE ***SPAM-FREE BOOK RELEASE NEWSLETTER***, AFTER WHICH YOU'LL IMMEDIATELY BE SENT A FREE COPY OF LUKE SMITHERD'S STORY ***THE JESUS LOOPHOLE***. AND IF YOU'RE THE SOCIAL MEDIA TYPE, FOLLOW ME ON TWITTER @LUKESMITHERD OR LIKE MY FACEBOOK PAGE "LUKE SMITHERD BOOK STUFF!"

Author's Afterword:

(Note: at the time of writing, any comments made in this afterword about the number of other available books written by me are all true. However, since writing this, many more books might be out!)

When it was first conceived, this story was notably different.

Long-term Smithereens (a fan name made up by someone, presumably some *genius* who coined such a wonderful phrase for my small-but-growing legionette of extremely mildly rabid fans... like, if one of them bit you, it'd hurt, but you wouldn't need a shot. You'd probably just need a sit down and a cookie while you waited for the easily resistible urge to buy one of my books to pass) may remember me mentioning, way back in the afterword of *In The Darkness, That's Where I'll Know You* (or rather in Part Four of that book when it was released in sections) that I was going to start work on a story called *Everyone Is Your Killer.* Remember that? No? Oh... so you're new here then. Well, hello! Welcome to the Smithereen collective. Kind of like the Borg, except resistance is not only anything *but* futile, but is in fact highly recommended.

Before I get into what happened to the original idea – in case you stop reading this right now – let me say a sincere thank you for reading this book. I really, really hope you enjoyed it. If you did, it would mean a huge deal to me if you could leave a star rating on Amazon before you forget. Although this is my first book to be actually published – in audio format at least, by Audible themselves who have been excellent to me – in print terms, I am still very much a self-published author and a minor name indeed, at least at the time of writing. Therefore, an absolutely huge part of my career is due to people who have been kind enough to leave those star ratings on Amazon (or even better, on Amazon USA *and* UK) as those star ratings are what convince people who have never heard of me (i.e.: most people) to try my work. If you could leave yours, it would be a massive, massive help, and if you do it before my next book comes out, *your* reviewer name will go in the Acknowledgements section of that book. And believe me, I see every single one. I check for them often enough. Either way, thank you for reading.

If you didn't enjoy the story, then as ever, I'm genuinely sorry about that. I wrote it the way I thought was best. Thank you anyway for trying it.

So, back to *Everyone Is Your Killer.* That story idea also featured the Man in White; from *The Stone Man* to *In The Darkness* to every story in *Weird. Dark.,* the ideas for the things I write always start with an image in my head, one that's as clear as day. With *The Stone Man,* it was one of Caementum himself coming out of the sea (although he didn't end up coming from the sea.) With *Kill Someone,* it was the image of a grinning Man in White standing on the doorstep of my parents' house, a bright sunny day behind him. The story always started there.

In the original idea, Chris was told that someone was coming to kill him, and that it would happen at any time. His job was to defend himself, and kill that person first if possible. He was told that this person had also taken several sisters prisoner, and that if he *didn't* take the other guy out, then they would all die. (Other than the sisters element, that story may still be written, so don't even fucking think about stealing it. I like the idea.)

Then the story changed, and the other guy was taken out. It would just be the sisters, abducted and threatened with a brutal death unless Chris accepts the challenge before him. Then one of them was going to be left in Chris' house, tagged in the same way Chris was, to be a constant pleading voice to get the murder job done.

Then I had the idea that halfway through the story—once the setup was the same as the story you've just read—the other 'coming to kill you' guy would be introduced as an extra level of hassle for Chris to deal with. But as tempting as that was, I nixed it; it didn't feel right for the story. The concept was what the concept was. Suddenly switching what the story was about felt like cheating. So that idea was removed, as was the girl in the house. Klaus, of course, was in all iterations of this story. He's probably not someone you would ever like to know, but I like that guy for some reason. And I'm pretty sure he was in *A Head Full of*

Knives, working for Rougeau, hidden under a balaclava. And yes, I think he did like Chris. But here's the funny thing:

When I started writing this, I had no idea who Chris was actually going to kill. I'd forgotten that I didn't know at first. I found a note just now that I'd written once I'd started the book: 'could Chris kill one of the girls?' That idea had totally clicked for me, and for the character, and more importantly for the themes of the book.

You may disagree. You may think Chris is stupid for not taking options A1 to Z12. But as Chris himself says, you aren't him. You're probably smarter than he is. But if you're going through the options in your own head and coming up with better ones, *then I've achieved exactly what I wanted to do.*

Regarding his choices, if it's any excuse, as I say I didn't know what Chris was going to do. I knew what the Man in White was up to all along, and how the story would end, but the victim was always in question at first. Chris figured his target out for himself. And if that sounds like awfully pretentious writer talk, then I agree, but I can't help it. This is a story that, for me, wrote itself. It started off as something that I thought was going to be a novella and then turned out to be something much bigger than that. Personally, I'm very pleased with the way it came out. For me, it's a realistic thriller, not a Hollywood thriller, and that's the way I like it. I imagine that there will be many that would prefer it to be the other way round, and I get it, but that's just not the kind of thing I like to write. There are enough of those already, and they're very good, but I want to try and do something new. I hope I succeeded.

If you're asking if I would kill someone in Chris' situation, then I think I would (as in, I would believe it to be the right thing to do... whether I *could* or not is another matter, and a question I profoundly hope I never have to answer.) I've had early readers who have said they just wouldn't do it. If you're asking me *who* I would kill—in order to save five other people—then off the top of my head, I would absolutely kill the guy in the pub toilet, kids or not. Other than that, I'd murder Matt Shaw.

By the way, other than the racial abuse – as I'm white – Chris' story from the bowling alley is taken from my real life, my Mum's presence included.

As I mentioned, this book is being published—and more importantly, marketed, as that has been the thing I have always been lacking on a major scale—by Audible. As such, it is the biggest break of my career, and I can't tell you how excited I am about that, and how much I can't wait to see where that leads. This might be a big step-up for me. About three years ago I was asked where I saw myself on the scale of being a writer, 1 being absolutely new and utterly self-published and no one knowing about me, and 10 being Stephen King. Three years ago I thought I was a 3. Now I'd say I'm about a 4. This might make me a 5. Fingers crossed. A big thank you to Sophie, Henna, and Laurence at Audible for making this happen and for all the support you've given to my self-published audio work.

How To Be A Vigilante: A Diary came out a few days ago, and this is the second book of mine other than that to feature no supernatural or Twilight Zone elements whatsoever. However, I'd like to think that it's still weird enough – or at least otherworldly enough – to keep my regular readers happy. Hey, if Mr. King can skip back and forth from *The Shining* to *Misery* to *11 22 63* to *Mr. Mercedes,* then I can do that too. Or at least try.

Lastly, as always, you can keep up with all Smitherd-related goings-on by liking Luke Smitherd Book Stuff on Facebook or following @lukesmitherd on Twitter, but if you *really* want to make sure you don't miss any new releases (and the chance to get books not only before they're released but for *free,* sign up for Luke Smitherd's Spam-Free Book Release Newsletter at lukesmitherd.com. If you do, you instantly get a free copy of my story *The Jesus Loophole* sent straight to your inbox. Pretty good, right? (The answer is 'yes.') It comes out only when there is genuine news and absolutely does not bombard you with emails as I hate that myself and wouldn't want to inflict it on anyone else.

Incidentally, you may have noticed a list of Smithereens With Titles in the acknowledgements section of this book (situated at the start and on the very last page). Want one yourself? Okay, you freakin' weirdo, you can have one; just drop me an email and tell me what you want, and you'll go in the next acknowledgements section too. Only rules are you have to keep it small; we had to change it after a few people went power mad, which to be fair is the default Smithereen mindset. No entire cities or states or countries can be under your dominion any more, as that wouldn't be fair to other people that live there and might want a title...

While I'm here, I might as well mention that Matt Shaw and I have a podcast called, *"Are You Sure? With Smitherd and Shaw"*, that comes out every two weeks. It's very silly, a lot of fun, and every week we go through the pros and cons of various topics, as well as scintillating intellectual features such as "Did You Meet A Dickhead This Week?" I'm sure the Sony award is in the post. Check us out on iTunes, Soundcloud, and Stitcher. I'd start after Episode 6 if I were you.

What's next, you might ask? For the first time in writing these afterwords, I have no idea. I have a list in my phone of book ideas, but at this stage – knowing the mountain of redrafts that still have to be done of this book, and with it following so soon on the heels of *HTBAV:AD* (we use a lot of acronyms in Smithereen land, and that's the first one with a colon we've ever had) my brain is a bit fried. We'll see. The funny thing is I'm writing this while sitting in a very cheap motel in Arizona the same one in which I wrote a lot of *Hold On Until Your Fingers Break.* That was one of my favourite writing memories ever, sitting on my room's porch with my freshly-bought little Bose speaker, a small but crappy bucket of Angry Orchard cider on ice sitting on the table next to me while the sun finished setting. Today I have a shittier room, and I'm writing this in the lobby because it's 104 outside even in the shade, and all that's on the table is a bottle of Smart Water and my sweated-up socks because it was too hot to wear them. But life is still pretty damn good right now. I have an actual writing career. Crazy, isn't it? I still have to pinch myself when I think back to the way things were when I first started. I've said this a lot, but it's true: nothing would have changed if not for you guys with your reviews and shares and support. Thank you *so* much.

Until next time, when the story will—I say this with a fairly high level of certainty—be taking a turn towards the impossible again. Watch this space.

Stay Hungry,

Luke Smitherd

Scottsdale, Arizona

September 18th, 2016

And now for a freebie, as promised: the beginning of Luke Smitherd's biggest selling novel, The Stone Man, *shortlisted for Audible UK's Book of the Year 2015 and available now in all formats on Amazon and Audible:*

The Stone Man

By Luke Smitherd

Chapter One: Andy at the End, The Stone Man Arrives, A Long Journey Begins On Foot, And the Eyes of the World Fall Upon England

***

The TV is on in the room next door; the volume is up, the news is on, and I can hear some Scottish reporter saying that it's about to happen all over again. I already knew that, of course, just like everyone watching already knows that 'The Lottery Question' is being asked by people up and down the country, and around the world. Who will it be this time?

That was my job, of course, although I won't be doing it anymore. That's why I'm recording this, into the handheld digi-dicta-doodad that Paul sent me after the first lot of business that we dealt with. To get it all out if you need to, he'd said (he knows I find it hard to talk to people. He thought talking to the machine might be easier. Plus, getting it all out now gives me an excuse to use it after all; feels strange holding one again, as if my newspaper days were decades ago instead of just a year or so).

I didn't really know what he was talking about, back then. It had hit him a lot harder than me, so I didn't really understand why I'd need to talk about it. Eventually I got it, of course … after the second time.

That was worse. Much worse.

This room is nice anyway, better than the outside of the hotel would suggest. I actually feel guilty about smoking in here, but at this stage I can be forgiven, I'm sure. Helps me relax, and naturally, I've got the entire contents of the mini bar spread out in front of me. I haven't actually touched any of it yet, but rest assured, I expect I shall have consumed most of it by the time I finish talking.

I just thought that I should get the real version down while I still have time. Not the only-partially-true, Home Office approved version that made me a household name around the world. I'm not really recording this for anyone else to hear, as daft as that may sound. I just think that doing so will help me put it all in perspective. I might delete it afterwards, I might not … I think I will. Too dangerous for it to get out, for now at least.

I'd obviously had to come here in disguise (amazing how much a pair of subtle sunglasses and a baseball cap let you get away with in summer) and it's a good job that I did. They'd already be up here, banging on the door, screaming about the news and telling me what I already know. Thanks to my disguise, I can sit quietly in this designer-upholstered, soft-glow, up-lit, beige yuppie hidey-hole, with Steely Dan playing in the background on my phone's speakers (sorry if you aren't a fan) and remain undisturbed, until ... well, until I'm done. And it's time.

This is for you as well, Paul; for you more than anyone. You were there for all of it, and you're a key player, not that you'll ever actually get to hear this.

Well, actually, you weren't there at the start, were you? I often forget that. Which, of course, would be the best place to begin. Heh, would you look at that; I just did an automatic segue. Still got all the old newsman moves. Slick ...

Sorry, I was miles away for a moment there. Remembering the first day. How excited those people were. Everybody knew it was something big.

Nobody was frightened. Not at first.

***

It was summer. Summer meant more people out shopping, eyeing up the opposite sex, browsing, meeting friends, having outdoor coffees and watered-down beer. In Coventry, the chance to do this (with the sun out, and not a single cloud visible in the sky on a weekend no less) was as rare as rocking-horse shit, and so there were more people out and about in the city centre than at pretty much any other time of the year. I sometimes wonder if this was the reason that particular day was picked; attracted to the mass of people perhaps? Or maybe it was just sheer chance.

I was stuck indoors for the earlier part of that day, and that was just fine by me. One, because I've never been a person who enjoys being out in harsh sunlight (makes me squint, I sweat easily, I burn easily, I can't stand it when my clothes stick to me ... need I go on? Sun worshippers doing nothing but sitting in sunlight; I'll never understand them) and two, because I was interviewing a local girl group ('Heroine Chic'; I shit you not) who were just about to release their debut piece-of-crap single. And it was awful, truly awful (I don't mean to come across as someone's dad, but it really was an assault on the ear drums. Middle-class white girls talking in urban patois. Exactly as bad as it sounds) but, at the time, I was still just on the right side of thirty-five, and so considered myself in with a chance of charming at least one of the trio; a stunning-looking blonde, brunette and redhead combo in their early twenties whose management were clearly banking on their looks to get them by, rather than their output. None of us knew it back then, but even that wouldn't be enough to help 'Get Into Me' (again, I shit you not) crack the top forty. Two more non-charting efforts later, Heroine Chic would find themselves back in obscurity before fame had found them; of the six of us in that room, including their enormous security guard and their wet-behind-the-ears looking manager, only one of us was destined to be known worldwide. None of us could have ever guessed that it would be me.

Not that I didn't have high hopes of my own in those days, lazy—but earnest—dreams of a glorious career in my chosen field. Obviously, the likes of Charli, Kel and Suze weren't going to land me a job at Rolling Stone, but I was starting to get good feedback on freelance pieces that I'd written for the Observer and the Times, and was listed as a contributor at the Guardian; I'd finally started to believe that in a year or two, I'd leave behind the features department at the local rag and then make my way to London to start shaking things up. I actually said that to colleagues as well: I'm gonna shake things up. That's how I often find myself talking to people, using sound bites and stagey lines to make an impression. As the interview drew to a close, and their manager started making 'wrap it up' signals while looking nervously at his smartphone, the girls and I posed together for a brief photo by the office window. They pouted, and I grinned honestly, enjoying the moment despite receiving zero interest from any of them. I made myself feel better by putting it down to the age gap.

They left with an all-too-casual goodbye, their bouncer blocking them all from view as they made their way to the escalator. I was done for the day—I'd only come in for the late afternoon interview, with it being a weekend—and it was approaching five, so the temperature would soon be dropping nicely into that relaxing summer evening feel that I actually like. I had no plans, and flatmate Phil had his brother over for the weekend. He was a good guy, and his brother a good guest, but I didn't particularly want to be stuck at home listening to the two of them endlessly discussing rugby. I decided that I'd maybe find a beer garden and have a read for an hour or so. In my twenties, this would have been that magical exciting hour where you'd text around and find out who was available for an impromptu session. No one was anymore.

I grabbed my bag and headed out of the building, thinking about possibly getting a bite to eat as well—although I intended to have something healthy, as lately the gym hadn't really been graced with my presence, and it was starting to show—and for some reason, I decided to stroll towards Millennium Place.

It used to be a big open-air space, a modern plaza designed for concerts and shows of all kinds. None of it's there anymore, of course; after the Second Arrival they dug it all up and put a small lake in its place, to see if it made any difference.

For some reason I was in a good mood and—in the words of the song—having 'no particular place to go', I thought I'd take a look at the summer crowds at Millennium Place, and then decide my destination from there, giving me time to work up an appetite. I people-watched as I went, passing barely dressed young couples who made me feel old and think about past opportunities of my own. I realised that the tune I'd been humming was 'Get Into Me'. I laughed out loud—I remember that distinctly—as I turned the corner and saw Millennium Place fully. When I saw what was going on, the laughter trailed off in my throat.

I suppose that I must have heard the commotion as I'd drawn closer; I'd been so lost in thought that somehow it didn't really register, or possibly I just subconsciously wrote it off as the usual summer crowd sound. But this was different. Around two hundred people were gathered in a cluster near the centre of Millennium Place, and there was an excited, confused buzz coming from them, their mobiles held out and snapping away at something in their midst. Other people were hanging back from them, getting footage of the crowd itself. That was the other reason I wanted to get into the big leagues, of course; everyone was a reporter in the digital age, and local print was shrinking fast.

I couldn't make out what was in the centre of the crowd, standing at a distance as I was, but I could see other people on the outskirts of the plaza having the same response as me; what's going on, whatever it is I want to see it. Don't misunderstand me, at this stage it was surprising and intriguing, but nothing really more than that; a chance for hopeful people to capture some footage that might go viral. You have to remember, none of us knew what it really was at that point. I assumed that it was somebody maybe doing some kind of street art, or perhaps a performance piece. That in itself was rare in Coventry, so in my mind I already had one hand on my phone to give Rich Bell—the staff photographer—a call, to see if he was available to get some proper photos if this turned out to be worth it. Either way, I walked towards the hubbub. As I got closer I could hear two people shouting frantically, almost hysterically, sounding as though they were trying to explain something.

The voices belonged to a man and a woman, and while I couldn't yet make out what they were saying, I could hear laughter from some listeners and questions from others; my vision was still mainly blocked by the medium-sized mass of bodies, but I could see that there was something fairly large in the middle of them all, rising just slightly above the heads of the gathered crowd and standing perfectly still.

I reached the cluster of people, now large enough to make it difficult to get through (to the point where I had to go on tiptoe to get a clear view) and that was the moment that I became one of the first few hundred people on Earth to get a look at the Stone Man.

Of course, it didn't have a name then. I'd like to tell you that I was the one who came up with it, but I'm afraid that would be a lie. As you may know, I was one of the people who really brought it into the common parlance worldwide, but I'd actually overheard it being used on a random local radio station as Paul and I raced through Sheffield later on (obviously, more on that to come) and thought it perfect, but I'd never actually intended to rip it off. By the point I was in front of the cameras, I'd used it so often that I'd forgotten that it wasn't a common term at the time.

It stood at around eight feet tall (to my eyes at least; the Home Office can give you the exact measurements) and it made me think then, as it does now, of the 'Man' logo on a toilet door, if someone were to make one out of rough, dark, greyish-brown stone and then mutate it so the arms were too long, and the head were more of an oval than a circle. The top half of its body was bent slightly forward as well, but the biggest departure from the toilet picture was that this figure had hands, of a sort; its arms tapered out at the ends, reminding me of the tip of a lipstick.

The most intriguing thing was, there was also an extremely quiet sound emanating from it. The best way I can describe it is as a bass note so low as to be almost inaudible. They still haven't figured that one out.

Now that I was closer, I could hear what one of the ranting people was saying. It was the woman, stood about ten feet away from me on the inside of the circle of gathered people. Based on the distance between the crowd, herself, and the Stone Man, it looked to me as if she was the reason they were hanging back from the hulking figure, and not swarming forward to touch and prod it.

She was patrolling back and forth in front of the Stone Man, wide-eyed and breathing heavily. If she wasn't keeping the people around her at bay deliberately, she was still doing a damn good job of it.

***

Continued in The Stone Man *by Luke Smitherd, available on Amazon and Audible! And please, if you feel so inclined ... leave your star rating for* Kill Someone *on Amazon before you forget!* ☺

Also By Luke Smitherd:

WEIRD. DARK.

PRAISE FOR *WEIRD. DARK.:*

"WEIRD and DARK, yes, but more importantly ... exciting and imaginative. Whether you've read his novels and are already a fan or these short stories are your first introduction to Smitherd's work, you'll be blown away by the abundance of ideas that can be expressed in a small number of pages." - Ain't It Cool News.com

Luke Smitherd is bringing his unique brand of strange storytelling once again, delivered here in an omnibus edition that collects four of his weirdest and darkest tales:

MY NAME IS MISTER GRIEF: what if you could get rid of your pain immediately? What price would you be prepared to pay?

HOLD ON UNTIL YOUR FINGERS BREAK: a hangover, a forgotten night out, old men screaming in the street, and a mystery with a terrible, terrible answer ...

THE MAN ON TABLE TEN: he has a story to tell you. One that he has kept secret for decades. But now, the man on table ten can take no more, and the knowledge - as well as the burden - is now yours.

EXCLUSIVE story, THE CRASH: if you put a dent in someone's car, the consequences can be far greater - and more strange - than you expect.

Available in both paperback and Kindle formats on Amazon and as an audiobook on Audible.

Also By Luke Smitherd:

The Stone Man

The #1 Amazon Horror Bestseller

Two-bit reporter Andy Pointer had always been unsuccessful (and antisocial) until he got the scoop of his career; the day a man made of stone appeared in the middle of his city.

This is his account of everything that came afterwards and what it all cost him, along with the rest of his country.

The destruction, the visions ...the dying.

Available in both paperback and Kindle formats on Amazon and as an audiobook on Audible.

Also By Luke Smitherd:

The Physics of the Dead

What do the dead do when they can't leave ... and don't know why?

The afterlife doesn't come with a manual. In fact, Hart and Bowler (two ordinary, but dead men) have had to work out the rules of their new existence for themselves. It's that fact—along with being unable to leave the boundaries of their city centre, unable to communicate with the other lost souls, unable to rest in case The Beast should catch up to them, unable to even sleep—that makes getting out of their situation a priority.

But Hart and Bowler don't know why they're there in the first place, and if they ever want to leave, they will have to find all the answers in order to understand the physics of the dead: What are the strange, glowing objects that pass across the sky? Who are the living people surrounded by a blue glow? What are their physical limitations in that place, and have they fully explored the possibilities of what they can do?

Time is running out; their afterlife was never supposed to be this way, and if they don't make it out soon, they're destined to end up like the others.

Insane, and alone forever ...

Available in both paperback and Kindle formats on Amazon and as an audiobook on Audible.

Also By Luke Smitherd:

IN THE DARKNESS, THAT'S WHERE I'LL KNOW YOU

What Is The Black Room?

There are hangovers, there are bad hangovers, and then there's waking up someone else's head. Thirty-something bartender Charlie Wilkes is faced with this exact dilemma when he wakes to find finds himself trapped inside The Black Room; a space consisting of impenetrable darkness and a huge, ethereal screen floating in its centre. Through this screen he is shown the world of his female host, Minnie.

How did he get there? What has happened to his life? And how can he exist inside the mind of a troubled, fragile, but beautiful woman with secrets of her own? Uncertain whether he's even real or if he is just a figment of his host's imagination, Charlie must enlist Minnie's help if he is to find a way out of The Black Room, a place where even the light of the screen goes out every time Minnie closes her eyes...

Previously released in four parts as, "The Black Room" series, all four parts are combined in this edition. In The Darkness, That's Where I'll Know You starts with a bang and doesn't let go. Each answer only leads to another mystery in a story guaranteed to keep the reader on the edge of their seat.

THE BLACK ROOM SERIES, FOUR SERIAL NOVELLAS THAT UNRAVEL THE PUZZLE PIECE BY PIECE, NOW AVAILABLE IN ONE COLLECTED EDITION:

IN THE DARKNESS, THAT'S WHERE I'LL KNOW YOU

Available in both paperback and Kindle formats on Amazon and as an audiobook on Audible.

Also By Luke Smitherd:

A HEAD FULL OF KNIVES

Martin Hogan is being watched all the time. He just doesn't know it yet. It started a long time ago too, even before his wife died. Before he started walking every day.

Before the walks became an attempt to find a release from the whirlwind that his brain has become. He never walks alone, of course, although his 18-month old son and his faithful dog, Scoffer, aren't the greatest conversationalists.
Then the walks become longer. Then the *other* dog starts showing up. The big white one, with the funny looking head. The one that sits and watches Martin and his family as they walk away.

All over the world, the first attacks begin. The Brotherhood of the Raid make their existence known; a leaderless group who randomly and inexplicably assault both strangers and loved ones without explanation.

Martin and the surviving members of his family are about to find that these events are connected. Caught at the center of the world as it changes beyond recognition, Martin will be faced with a series of impossible choices ... but how can an ordinary and broken man figure out the unthinkable? What can he possibly do with a head full of knives?

Luke Smitherd (author of the Amazon bestseller THE STONE MAN and IN THE DARKNESS, THAT'S WHERE I'LL KNOW YOU) asks you once again to consider what you would do in his unusual and original novel. A HEAD FULL OF KNIVES is a supernatural mystery that will not only change the way you look at your pets forever, but will force you to decide the fate of the world when it lies in your hands.

Available in both paperback and Kindle formats on Amazon and as an audiobook on Audible.

Also By Luke Smitherd:

He Waits – A Book of Strange and Disturbing Horror

Praise for HE WAITS:

"In the horror genre, familiarity absolutely does breed contempt, and Smitherd obviously knows this. Why else would he be so talented at expertly crafting stories that defy expectations? For me there is no greater joy than seeing an artist excel at his craft." - *Aintitcoolnews.com*

In *HE WAITS*, Luke Smitherd brings you two more Tales Of The Unusual ...

Quite literally, no escape. Because he's always with you. And in the real world - the world of you, the reader - HE WAITS will stay in your mind in a way that you won't expect ...

PLUS THE SECOND STORY, 'KEEP YOUR CHILDREN CLOSE':

A campsite. A family holiday. A broken down car. And an approaching breakdown truck that is just the start of Shelley's nightmare. By the time the sun sets, someone in that field will be dead, and Shelley must somehow make sure it isn't one of her children ... KEEP YOUR CHILDREN CLOSE is a story that you will find impossible to predict.

Available now in the Amazon Kindle Store

Also By Luke Smitherd:
How to be a Vigilante: A Diary

In the late 1990s, a laptop was found in a service station just outside of Manchester. It contained a digital journal entitled 'TO THE FINDER: OPEN NOW TO CHANGE YOUR LIFE!' Now, for the first time, that infamous diary is being published in its entirety.

It's 1998. The internet age is still in its infancy. Google has just been founded.

Eighteen-year-old supermarket shelf-stacker Nigel Carmelite has decided that he's going to become a vigilante.

There are a few problems: how is he going to even find crime to fight on the streets of Derbyshire? How will he create a superhero costume - and an arsenal of crime-fighting weaponry - on a shoestring budget? And will his history of blackouts and crippling social inadequacy affect his chances?

This is Nigel's account of his journey; part diary, part deluded self-help manual, tragically comic and slowly descending into what is arguably Luke Smitherd's darkest and most violent novel.

What do you believe in? And more importantly ...should you?

Available in both paperback and Kindle formats on Amazon and as an audiobook on Audible.

Printed in Great Britain
by Amazon